Maggie
Best of [illegible]
Felicity

Full Circle

by

Felicity Edwards

Published 2023

Acknowledgements

The author would like to thank the members of the Dean Writers Circle, plus the beta readers, for their invaluable input.

Also, many thanks to Baker of Plan B Associates for the stunning cover.

Dedication

To my faithful muses O and K

Chapter 1

A Bone and a Cave

It was early spring when the shadow fell over man and lamb. The hawk swooped, talons at the ready. Ivan leapt up, waving his arms and yelling, "Go away."The little lamb frolicked about Ivan's feet moments before now experienced a double dose of terror. Human yelling and the shadow of death. It ran helter-skelter towards the undergrowth of the boundary. Bleating frantically, it pushed through the barrier and tumbled down the slope. Instinctively running for his life, he headed for shelter and found it. He called for his human carer, "Ivan, come and rescue me! I'm where no flying death comes."

Could Ivan find it?

Ivan climbed down the slope to an old unused path leading to the river. His worry was the lamb might reach the water's edge.

The lamb's bleats sounded closer. At least it had not got to the river, but where was it? He knew it had to be nearby, yet he could not see it. He pushed past a bush, and a thorn jabbed his finger. Pulling his hand back, he sucked the few drops of blood. A sheen of sweat soon appeared on his chin and forehead. Exasperated, he wiped his hand over his face smearing a line of blood across his cheek. He had to find this lamb. Reaching for the knife in his belt, he slashed at the hanging mass of greenery. Without warning, it gave way. He fell onto a soft dusty surface of what he presumed to be a cave. He heard the bleat clearly now. The hole in the green curtain let in a thin shaft of light. He peered into the dim interior but could not make out the end. Sniffing the air reassured him since the rank odour of a predator's home was absent, but where was the lamb? Ivan worried in case there was a hibernating bear in the dark interior. Would the bleating wake it? At the thought, he felt a wave of terror and fumbled in his pockets until he located a box of matches. The momentary flare of the match failed to show where the lamb had wandered. As a comfort more than anything else, he muttered. "Lambkin, show me where you are. This must be a huge cave. I can hear you but not see you."

On cue, the lamb bleated again. Leaving the half-light of the entrance, Ivan moved slowly towards the sound. Then he sneezed. His footsteps were causing clouds of dust to rise. He made out the shape of the lamb and felt a wave of relief. But as he reached to pick it up, his fingers brushed against something hard. Holding tight to the lamb, he lit another match to see what they had disturbed. The light soon blinked out but not before he saw a bone lying on the ground. Another match confirmed the object to be a large bone. One, he recognised it as a human bone.

Worried, he said, "Oh, little one, what have you brought us to now?" He thought it looked like a human thigh bone, but a huge one.

He spoke aloud to quell his rising fear, "I wonder where this has come from?" Holding the lamb close, like a child's teddy bear, he bent down and carefully picked up the bone, trying to shake some dirt off.

"Well, my little friend, you're lucky. Although the light

is dim here, I can't see any tooth marks of a predator." He wondered if it could be from a long-forgotten murder victim or possibly some vagrant from ages ago who came in here to seek shelter from the cold winter and maybe died from hypothermia. After all, communications were unreliable in this northwestern part of Siberia up in the Altai Mountains, and anything could happen. In his view, this would be a perfect place to hide a body. But where were the rest of the bones if that was the case? He shuddered and dropped it onto the soft soil. He felt goose pimples rising on his arms and across the nape of his neck. He did not know why he felt scared. Holding the lamb tight to his chest, he crooned to it, more to still his pounding heart than any distress the little animal might still be feeling. He felt oddly unsettled and decided this was no place to linger.

Fear drove him rapidly forward to the edge of the cave without pausing. Ducking through the gap, he stared back up the slope. No ghosts followed. Still terrified, he fled through the hedge and back to the rest of the flock. His heart still pounding and shaking uncontrollably, he rounded the flock and hastily drove them to their warm shed behind the farmyard. Once safely inside, an upturned bucket served as a seat until he regained his breath and his heart returned to its usual slow beat.

Anxious about the effects on the lamb, he grabbed a bottle and fed it. Ivan had helped at the birth. It had been long, and he had assisted the little creature, but the mother took one look at the weak, spindly-legged thing, hardly able to stand, and walked away. She refused to let it feed, so Ivan had taken over its care. Bottle feeding was the simple bit. Keeping it warm was a struggle until the farmer's wife suggested he wrap the scrawny creature in an old blanket and place it in the oven of the old kitchen range with the door open or in a box beside if she had been cooking. He woke day and night to feed it, and instead of dying, as everyone expected, it thrived. It followed Ivan everywhere. Ivan wondered if the other sheep bullied it because of its privileged position. At least now, it lived in the shed with the rest of the flock. Once he was sure his charges were safe and fed, he slowly shut the doors and balled his hands into fists as he made his way back to the farmhouse to report the incident to the farmer

The following day, the young shepherd checked for a way back to the cave to show the farmer and a tall, thick-set police officer the "bone cave". With his bullet-shaped head, narrowed eyes, and pursed lips, the tall officer glowered and looked down on the lad. Although he had only come from the local village, he was not pleased and wore a permanent scowl. This time they had torches, so reaching the back of the cave and the bone was quicker. The police officer played the light over the high ceilings and walked to the end of the cave. There branching off to the right were two passages, a narrow one continuous with the cave's back wall and another much broader set in front of the narrow one. He played his torch over all the rocky surfaces. There did not appear to be anything that looked like a body or more bones. Neither could he see any signs of habitation. He questioned Ivan, "Now, young Yezhov, are you sure you didn't see any other bones here? There must have been more."

Scared, as any seventeen-year-old would be, at being questioned like this, Ivan shook his head, "No, sir, I didn't see any other bones. I only had a match for light, and their light doesn't last long."

Harrumphing, the officer glared at him. Once again, he shone his torch around, marvelling at the height of the ceilings. Seeing no other bones, he bent and picked up the lonely bone in gloved hands, dropped it into a plastic evidence bag, and glared at the shepherd as if he was the guilty party. He sighed. He had nothing more to do here and stalked off.

Some weeks later, the farmer called Ivan, "Don't leave the yard. I've asked Piotr to cover for you today. Someone is coming to look at the cave, and they'll need you to take them there."

When the vehicle drove up to the farmhouse, he saw it was a woman driving. He guessed her to be in her early forties. She leapt down and called to him simultaneously as she fixed her long, fair hair in a ponytail poking from under a light blue cap.

"Hi, are you the guy who found that cave with the bone?"

He nodded, the power of speech had left him. He thought this was the prelude to being held and questioned by the police.

She thrust her hand out, "Hi, I'm Dr Sonja Sokolov. I'm an archaeologist and wondered if you could show me to this cave? I've already spoken to your employer, who said you would take me there."

Now he understood why he had to stay in the yard. He breathed a great sigh of relief and offered to help as Sonja had brought strong lights. Together they struggled down the rough track. After setting the lights where she wanted, she carefully looked and felt over all the surfaces. She paid particular attention to the side chambers.

At last, she nodded and sighed. Turning to him, she said, "Thanks for your help. This cave looks promising. They returned hours later. He was anxious about his flock. The archaeologist was filthy but smiled happily. She thanked the farmer, "I need to speak to my university and some of my associates from other universities too. I'll contact you when I know what we can do. It looks like this could be a potential site for exploration. That bone is a significant find. This might be a neolithic burial site."

The farmer nodded, he hadn't a clue what neolithic was, but if the university wanted to come, they would pay him handsomely.

Soon there was a well-worn pathway, and the cave was a hive of activity. Sonja had attracted the attention of many colleagues from all over the world. This project sounded so promising there was interest from many institutions. Some offered to fund a season, while others wanted to send some of their students as volunteers. They were all very excited since this was the first proof of human occupation at a much earlier date than previously supposed.

Ivan regularly visited to watch what was happening. Having been there at the onset, he felt a sense of ownership. Looking at what they were doing, Ivan asked, "Sonja, what are the trenches for, and why are people sifting the dirt?"

Sonja explained. "Each of the layers in the cave has a number. We are looking for the oldest level." She stretched and continued. "We think the bone you found is from the earliest level, but we can't figure out how it came to be on the surface since there were no signs of disturbance.

Now Ivan was even more intrigued. "Does the bone belong to a man or a woman?" Looking pensive, he asked. "Do you think the spirits in the cave put that bone there? Maybe they want us to find them or even set them free?"

She laughed, "Ivan, I'm a scientist. From the size, I think it could be a very tall man. To answer your question, I don't believe in spirits. I think nothing like that could happen, but in this profession, it's best to keep an open mind."

He replied, "I'm just a poor, uneducated shepherd boy. Maybe that's why I feel so odd every time I go into the cave. Maybe the spirits, or whatever, want to talk to me." He lifted his head and stared at her. "I'm sure there's a reason that bone suddenly appeared. Do spirits talk to us?"

She smiled indulgently, "I told you I don't know. I'll ask around at the university for the people who study things like that and get back to you."

Then they walked down to the cave and safer subjects in her mind.

The laboratory results for the dating of the bone came back and more than justified the excavation. It caused many an archaeologist to rethink the times of human existence. This bone was 34,000 years old, give or take a couple of thousand. At such a great age, scientists classified it as pre-human. Whoever these ancient beings were, from the bone, the scientists felt these people looked much like us today except taller.

Every day Ivan felt more drawn to these people. "Sonja, what kind of lives might they have led if they were like us?"

She creased her forehead and then said, "I don't know, but I suppose it would be like many other hunter-gatherer societies that exist even today. Since there was a global ice age, the climate must have been much harsher. Spring would still be cold, summer shorter than we have, and winter would be long and very cold. I imagine they would also be quite hungry most of the time."

Soon rumours swirled around, and once the press hounds heard, there were extravagant headlines that told nothing but promised much. Like this one from the Siberian Herald,

"Bone found by young shepherd could belong to a new giant race of humankind."

Ivan stood in the passage to the formally deserted back wing of the farmhouse. The transformation amazed Ivan. Now the musty furniture was gone instead. Instead, the bedrooms had bunk beds turning them into male and female dormitories. The silent old house came alive, filled with chattering students and labourers who came to work on the most exciting archaeological dig of the year, maybe even the century.

Once Sonja had informed him of the age of the bone, Ivan became convinced the spirits had moved it from their level, the deepest one, to the top. He felt sure they knew it was time for their people to be acknowledged. Every day after putting his flock into their accommodation, Ivan picked his way down the muddy path to the cave. He wanted to know what new things they had discovered. Now there were many people and a lot of activity, so Ivan was not afraid, but he still experienced that strange prickling sensation down the nape of his neck whenever he was in the cave. Sonja happily laid down her tools to tell him of their progress and show him their finds before carefully packing them to send to the university.

Sonja and her team worked in several trenches. The results from the one at the front of the cave were the most exciting. It yielded artefacts through most layers, showing an almost continuous occupation, including these elusive people, Neanderthals, and even homo sapiens. Most of the finds were the flakes of stone left after stone-knapping activities throughout the millennia of occupation. These little flakes would not be of much use but would have come from shaping more sophisticated stone tools. It was on a morning early in the week when one workman yelled. "Dr Sokalov, come and look. I think I've found something."

She hurried over and peered at the piece of flint, then carefully brushed all the dirt off and gasped, "This is an arrowhead. Which layer did you find it?"

She expected it to be in one of the more recent ones, but the worker showed her the deepest level. She shook her head. She was discovering these people were proving to be an enigma. First, the bone turned out to be even older than anyone thought. This showed the manufacturing to be so delicate it surpassed the skill of those she had seen at other sites and of later dates. She took great care to photograph and record the position, then left it to show Ivan when he visited in the evening before she sent it back to the laboratory for a more detailed examination.

Weeks later, the laboratory technicians informed Sonja that the arrowhead was not of local stone, nor did it match any of the stone knapping detritus in the cave. Suggesting the manufacturing would be elsewhere. After much searching, they identified the source for the flint was an area about 15 miles away.

The discovery intrigued Ivan when she told him about the area where the stone originated. On his day off, he persuaded his friend Vlad, who had a battered old truck, to take him to the site. They spent the whole day fossicking around and came across another three arrowheads with a similar design to the one in "his" cave.

By now, he knew to mark precisely where they found them and take photos on their phones. Sonja was thrilled with their interest and their finds. She happily paid both lads. Holding the money in her hand, she said, "Right guys, this is your payment for these finds, but I also want you to take me to the place you found them." She suspected finding three close together might indicate another cave in the vicinity. She asked, "While poking for these, did you see anything which might be another cave? It's possible other people made these."

Vlad and Ivan shook their heads. "Vlad said, "It's not a place we've been to before, but I don't remember any talk of a cave there." He turned to Ivan. "Have you?"

That did not stop them from planning to come and explore again. Ivan's day off became predictable. He made straight for the area and carefully searched. He poked and prodded any rock formations; his persistence finally paid off. Just before the end of summer, he discovered what he thought could be a cave. A rockfall years ago had all but obscured the entrance. He was with Vlad that day when they accidentally noticed the small aperture as their stick went into a hollow area behind a bush.

Once Ivan described the surroundings, and the proximity of the arrowhead finds to Sonja, she beamed with excitement. The next day she brought a couple of her team. They removed the bush and saw a small opening. Carefully they lifted the rocks out one by one and found an entrance. It was like opening the door to Aladdin's cave as there were signs of ancient habitation. Sonja felt a tremor of excitement. However, this late in the season, they only had time to do a quick search, but even that yielded a few artefacts which she hoped were of the same age as the older layers of the cave they were already excavating. They took a few of the items to date. They carefully sealed the cave as it was the end of the season and decided not to announce its discovery until next year. By then, the lab would have the dates for the artefacts. She would know if it was worth opening up a second site.

A peek into life 34,000 years ago.

Back in the mists of time, the people of the cave were busy. It was early spring, and there was much to prepare for the Burda trip. All the clans of the tribe travelled to the Burda site every other year, and this was that year. Not all the clan would go. The journey was arduous and not without its dangers. It was a significant event in their lives. Grievances that the shaman or the cave leader could not resolve would be dealt with by all the elders together. It was also the time for marriages and celebrations of births and deaths, acknowledging children's move into young adulthood after puberty rites and general social interactions. Also, it was when all the shamans, who were also the clan storytellers, would entertain the people. Since the clans had survived the rigours of the long cold winters, it was also the place and time to celebrate.

The old shaman of the cave and his son Guta were going together. Sometimes they tried to share the responsibilities, and one would stay home while one would travel. In one of their trance sessions, the spirits had spoken to them, demanding they both attend. They understood, for some reason, that it was important for both of them. Throughout the long winter, Guta's mother kept busy preparing new clothes for both the men and herself. She liked to decorate their tunics with little ostrich eggshell beads. The birds did not live near them, but one of the other caves further towards the east always brought the huge empty eggshells. On the occasions they had brought them with their contents, the cooked egg was always popular with the visitors, but the shells had to be saved. The bead makers were very good at drilling the tiny holes in the shell fragments, which the women rubbed on stones and fur to shape a little bead. First on rough rock, then moving onto smooth ones and finally polishing each one with a piece of rabbit skin which she kept for that purpose.

She smiled to herself as she worked. Guta hated all the fussy bits. He was quite happy to leave his tunic unadorned apart from the feathers, which were part of the shaman's dress, like their uniform.

Like many of those around, she was aware of the changes in their land. There were more incursions of what they called the New People. They were smaller and slight compared to the cave dwellers. They were quick-witted and were good at hunting but still relied on their legs to do the work. She glanced towards the entrance where their mounts kept out of the cold. Mostly they were wild but came to certain people on a specific whistle. Both her husband and Guta had horses. She did not need one, so she had never made friends or trained one. They took some of them to the Burda loaded with all the stuff they needed. Attaching two poles to the horses and a rawhide sling between them it formed a platform supporting the things they required while attending the Burda. The horses dragged the contraption along the ground. When they arrived, they used the poles as supports for their shelters. They used the same set-up when they went off to the summer hunting grounds.

There were signs the glaciers, which formed a backdrop to their lives, were melting. Guta's mother knew they all needed to go this year. They needed to discuss these and the effect it had on the tribes. The leaders thought that although these climatic changes were slow at the moment, they were sure they would bring about considerable changes in time to come.

Already groups were making plans to move to new hunting and living areas. One group had set off towards the setting sun only last year. Amongst their number was her cousin. She had always liked the young woman, although there was a big difference in their ages. She hoped they could still send messengers to report to the Burda elders.

Chapter 2

The Making of a Shaman

Every time Ivan went into the cave, he had a strange prickling sensation down the back of his neck as if someone was touching him. He would put his hand there, thinking it might be a spider, but nothing was there. Eventually, he wondered if it was the spirits calling him. All it did was make him feel very confused. At first, he was afraid to mention this idea, but eventually, he asked Sonja a general question to see if there was such a thing as spirit communication.

She smiled at him, "Yes, of course, there is, if you believe it. That's what shamans do all around the world."

It confused him, "What do you mean, shaman? Who are they? Are any alive now?"

"Yes, there are people who still believe in things like this. Why? What is troubling you?"

As he stood talking to her, he watched the tip of his shoe make marks in the dirt, "No, nothing is troubling me. I was just wondering, that's all."

The next time Sonja came out to the site, only a few days later. They were finding so many things in the cave site there was an urgent need for constant supervision. She had a few books, but before handing them to Ivan, she said, "I forgot to ask you, do you read?"

He looked affronted, "Yes, of course, I can read and write, but I had to leave at the end of my primary education. My parents could not afford to keep me at school, I needed to work, so I got this job as a shepherd. This way, I get all my meals at work, so most of my wages go to my parents to support my three little sisters. It makes a big difference to them. My boss, the farmer, lets me read some of his books, but most of them are about farming, and I don't think that's what I want to do for the rest of my life."

She thought about her own privileged life as an only child. Both her parents were academics. After some reflection, she decided to see if it were possible, from an educational point of view, to improve matters for him. Smiling while reaching into the vehicle and drawing out three books, she said, "I'm so pleased you can read as I brought these for you. I got them second-hand so that you can keep them. They are about shamans going into a trance and seeing or talking to the spirit world. It's not my cup of tea, but I thought you better know since you asked. When you have studied them, maybe you could explain shamanism to me. You might even get me interested!"

It thrilled him to own not one but three books. He smiled and held them reverently as they walked into the farmhouse kitchen. While Sonja chatted to the farmer's wife and sipped tea, he quietly went to his tiny room and tucked these most precious objects in his life into a big bag under his bed. The other lads must never know about these, or they would tease him and say he was getting above himself. The teasing was nothing to him, but he did want to improve himself, but they must not know.

As he returned to the kitchen, Sonja looked up, "Well, are we going to look at what is happening at the site?"

They talked of the many finds of more recent origin, but

he wanted to see if there were more from the deepest layers yet. The current objects were mainly stone tools from the different layers and a few small bones, nothing like that first bone find. However, it showed a continuous occupation for many millennia within the cave. He wondered what happened to "his" people. Were they ousted, or did they die out? He asked Sonja, and she replied she was an archaeologist for that he would need to talk to a paleoanthropologist.

Perplexed, he questioned her, "What? Why talk to them? They sound weird. What do they do? Will any ever come here?"

"Funny you should ask, one is coming next week, just to get a feel of the place. He is a friend of mine, I'll introduce you to him, and you can take him around and maybe ask about your lost cave people and even about shamans."

Every evening Ivan went to his freezing room to read his books, mainly by the light of a candle, since the electricity supply was very erratic. He kept a book in his bag, so while out with the sheep, he read whenever he had the chance. His favourite book was about training to be a shaman. It covered the different altered states of consciousness and the various shamanic pathways, but best of all, there were exercises to learn how to enter this thing called a shamanic state of consciousness. On reaching the pasture, he did a quick survey, ensuring there were no wolf or bear tracks. Once he considered the area safe, out would come the book, his concentration alternated between the flock and the book. He either read or practised the exercises, which, according to the text, would make him into a shaman in time. He wanted that to happen. Then he hoped he could help the spirits of the cave.

Ivan spoke to his friend Vlad. "I'm enjoying studying the books Sonja gave me, but I need help with some exercises. Would you be prepared to give me a hand?"

Vlad was intrigued by the changes in his friend. "Yes, of course, I'll do my best to help. What do you want?"

"Well, before we can do anything, we need a drum. I don't think there's a real one anywhere around here, so we'll have to make one."

They explored all the outbuildings for anything suitable. In the tractor shed, Vlad found an old paint tin without a lid, "Hey Ivan, look, I think that'll do just fine."

They banged it with a stick. It only produced a tinny sound. The lads pondered a bit, then Ivan smiled, "I know. Let's wrap the end of the stick with rags and see what happens."

It improved the sound, so they continued wrapping and testing until they had a bulbous end on the stick. It was very makeshift, but it gave the effect they wanted. Ivan said, "That's great. If you're free after work tomorrow evening, can you come over here, and we could give it a go?

The next evening when Vlad arrived, they quietly went out to the workshop where they had hidden their musical instrument. It was too cold to work in the fields, but they found a cosy corner in the old place and settled down.

Ivan instructed his friend, "I need you to keep up a constant beat. This drum beat is to help me go on a shamanic journey, not for you to become a rock star. We're lucky this room is nearly dark, so there's no need to do anything more to cut the light out. The book says there should be no light, but I'm sure this will do."

Vlad settled on an old tyre, "It better. I'm not sitting in total darkness banging a drum. That would make me feel like a complete and utter fool."

Ivan covered a wooden board on the floor with an old cloth. He told Vlad, "I'm going to lie here, and I want you to beat. If you time it on your phone after ten minutes, I need you to drum four beats fast. That'll signal me to return from the trance I'm hoping to go into."

Vlad's eyes were wide, "Are you sure this is safe? What if a monster comes up out of nowhere?"

Ivan smiled, "Vladislav Lazarev, now you are childish and silly. It's nothing like that. All I have to do is relax and visualise an opening into the earth. The book says the first journey is a simple exploration down through a tunnel into the lower world and maybe what lies beyond that. I want to become good at this to help those spirits in the cave."

Vlad nodded. He was happy to help his friend but scared about what might happen. He tentatively beat his new "drum," Once he had the rhythm of about 200 to 220 beats per minute, his friend nodded and lay on the board. His body relaxed as Ivan closed his eyes and took a few deep breaths. Following the instructions from the book, he visualised an opening into the earth, not the two caves they knew. Instead, he thought of a spring on the other side of the hills where he sometimes took his flock to drink. Concentrating on its appearance for a few minutes with the sound of Vlad beating the drum, Ivan imagined himself entering the spring. Suddenly he was passing through the water into a tunnel.

Strangely it felt as though he was moving fast, passing through concentric rings of light and dark. At first, they were circular, but then they became elliptical, but he was always in motion. It felt as if he was flying through a corrugated pipe. Slowly the vertical ellipses became more horizontal like an entrance, beyond which there was a grey landscape. It was like passing over an underground sea. Then came a sense of being directed to another tunnel and passing through the concentric circles again. He had a feeling he was pulsing with them. The change in the drumbeat's rhythm showed it was time to return. He wanted to stay longer but moved through the tunnel quickly. His body shuddered, and he took a deep breath as he slowly opened his eyes and looked at his friend.

Grinning, he broke the tension, "That was amazing. Thanks for your drumming."

Vlad gave a jerky laugh, "You had me worried there for a moment. Your eyes were closed but doing funny things moving quickly from side to side. Is that normal?"

"Yes, I think that shows the depth of the relaxation. It's what the book describes. It was amazing. I went down a tunnel-like corrugated pipe and then over an underground sea."

"Don't tell me anymore; it'll make me even more scared."

They went into the kitchen for a hot drink before Vlad returned home.

There was still a knot of students from the dig sitting around the big old table, "Hi, you guys, where have you been? We looked all over the place for you."

The lads looked at each other as Ivan answered, "Oh, we weren't doing much, just looking over some stuff out in the workshop."

Ivan studied every evening after work, reading how shaman all over the world serve their people, either to cure physical illness or mental conditions and to find answers to problems within their communities. He read they do this by entering an altered state of consciousness, which is like a trance state. They learn where to journey according to the problem. Ivan thought if he wanted to help the spirits in the cave first, he would need to know what they wanted. Why did they put the bone there to be found? And, of course, why him? He and Vlad decided they needed to practice together to get the drumming right, so there was always someone there to guide Ivan back using the drum beats when he needed to return from a journey.

His job enabled Ivan to appreciate his unique position. He could spend hours outdoors with the sheep giving him time to read and reflect, and now he had a friend who was happy to support him while he undertook these excursions into the lower and upper world of the spirits. He also knew he had time to seek the spirit animals and plants the book said would be needed to help him on his journeys. He knew he should enter this non-ordinary reality only for serious purposes, not play as Vlad had suggested, wanting to know silly things like the winning horse's name at the races so they could place a bet.

On his journeys into the other worlds, Ivan found he could appreciate a lot more about life and death. Most thrilling was when he understood he had conscious control over the directions of his travels. At the end of the month, Ivan visited the cave to attempt to contact the people of long ago. He knew it would be long before he could communicate with them, but being an invisible observer would help archaeologists like Sonja decide where to look for more evidence of these people.

On one of his journeys, he saw and understood some strange things were happening to "his" people. He watched and followed and understood the following scene, which he wrote about in his journal to describe to Sonja later.

The people from the deepest layer in the Cave

The messenger arrived, "There's a small group of the New People heading this way." He panted as he reached the top of the slope leading into the Cave. Guta and his father looked at each other. The older man nodded. They quietly motioned to Een, the cave leader, to join them. They walked deliberately to the top of the slope, Een carrying his spears. Once there, they whistled. Three horses appeared out of the swirling mist as if by enchantment. These impressive men easily hopped on the horses' backs and rode along the ridge, eventually coming to the promontory, which guarded the valley leading to their cave. They sat motionless on their horses. Een held his spear upright, resting on the ground.

They watched as a group of about twelve men who were the advance party of a tribe of the New people came into view. They were excellent hunters and trackers, but at first, not even they noticed the three watchers on the ridge. The mist swirled like a curtain opening. To their astonishment, three huge figures looked down on them. The New People were smaller than their watchers but brave. Their leader brandished his spear. The watchers did not move. They approached closer. Still, the watchers did not move. Now the incomers felt a prickling as the hairs rose on the nape of their necks and down their arms. Who were these watchers? Their eyes were so pale it was as if they were white, their pale bronze-coloured hair, long and floating in the breeze, held captive only by a headband. They had four legs like horses, but spears like they themselves carried only longer.

They had heard of powerful shamans living here. These horse people must be them. They wondered if their spear was just for decoration. Could they kill merely by looking? Whatever the case, they felt uncomfortable. The leader signalled they should leave. The others were grateful for his decision, and the whole group turned and hurried away. The tribe would make a long detour to avoid this area in the future.

Guta had a questioning look. The old man nodded, "They have gone for now. They will be back."

Een looked at the shaman, "How do you know they will be back? They looked pretty scared to me."

"That group might not come back, but their kind will. The Spirits said we are coming to the end of our time here."

Een looked confused, "But shouldn't we stop that from happening? My hunters could track and kill those puny-looking creatures."

Guta's father sighed. He was used to the immediacy of thinking of the hunters, "No, killing them won't make any difference. It is coming to the time for the puny ones to take over. They need us, though. When the time is ready, we will leave here and journey to all the parts of the world. We will teach and show those small skinny people how to live together. How to govern, and how to respect the wishes of the spirits. We will be scattered, but they need us to guide them. Then they will kill us."

"Not me. Such weak-looking people will not kill me!"

"No, not you personally, but our kind. The time is not here yet, I doubt you or I will see it, but it might happen for our children or grandchildren."

Silently they returned to their hearths.

Chapter 3

A Bead and Bone

Late Spring

Ivan was about to head out with the flock when Sonja arrived. She had a passenger who unfolded himself from the passenger seat, stretched and looked around. Ivan watched and thought the guy resembled an owl with big dark-rimmed glasses and a whispy reddish beard.

Sonja called. "Hi Ivan, I'm glad I caught you before you disappear like the Pied Piper." She indicated her companion. "This is Mikhail Konev. He is the man you need to talk to about spirit communications."

Ivan looked again at the guy. If this chap could help him in his mission to understand the cave spirit's needs, he would be very welcome.

Ivan said, "I'll leave the flock here for a bit while we go down to the cave."

The young lambs grew. It came closer to the time they sent the little rams off to the abattoir. By now, though, young Lambkin showed his affection for Ivan. He followed him around, more like a dog than a sheep. Feeding or settling to sleep close to Ivan. Their bond was such Ivan named him Bone.

"Please, Sir, I know it's time to send the rams off, but Bone has become more like a pet than a sheep. Please, could you consider letting him stay on the farm with me?"

The farmer looked at Ivan over the top of his glasses. "Since you and that animal has made this farm a famous place, I cannot complain. You may keep him, but I do not want that ram anywhere near my ewes when full-grown. If you want to become a sheep farmer, you must get sheep from other flocks."

So it became a familiar sight to see the youth followed by his sheep companion. He came when called and continued to head-butt his human friend to show his affection.

When Sonja heard Ivan was reading by candlelight, she presented him with a wind-up lantern. This light source allowed him to read late into the night. He still had to rise early but was so excited about the information from all the reading that tiredness was a small price to pay.

Meanwhile, Sonja thought about the lad. She was touched at his dogged determination to study the books she gave him. He showed her the journal he kept about his shamanic experiences. She sensed his potential to achieve more than just being a shepherd. She wondered if there was any way she could help. She thought about how easy her life had been, the only child of academic parents who encouraged her to study and do what she loved. Sonja spoke to her parents. "Dad, you know I told you about Ivan, who found the bone? Do you think there is any way we could offer him a place at the university to encourage his interest in archaeology?"

They were sitting at the dinner table, and her father rested his chin on his cupped hands, a favourite gesture when he was thinking. "I think there might be a way. I know we have a pre-study course for students with different educational backgrounds. Maybe I could speak to the board of governors and see if they would agree to let him undertake the course and the exams. If he passes, as with all the others, he could be automatically admitted to the university. He could study the course of his choice, in this case, Archaeology. You do realise with only primary school education, he would be hopelessly out of his depth. I'm not holding out much hope for his chances."

Sonja grinned. "You don't know him, but please, would you put his case forward?"

Weeks later, when they again met over coffee in the canteen, Sonja asked. "Well, have you had that meeting? What's the result?"

He smiled at her eagerness. "Yes, I have, and the answer is yes. If he studies the material they provide and sits the examination and if he passes, the university will admit him but only to study Archaeology."

Sonja arrived at the site excited with the news, but Ivan was still out with his sheep and not due until evening. She went to the cave site, leaving a request for him to come and see her as soon as he arrived back. The shadows were already lengthening before he looked around the site and saw her. She was right at the back, peering at the soil in one trench. He jumped down beside her and poked a finger at a little speck lighter than those around it, "What do you think that is?"

She jumped back, "Oh, it's you! Don't do that. You frightened me."

He smiled, "Why? Why are you afraid? You left a message for me, and here I am."

They looked at the speck he showed and carefully scraped the soil away from around it, eventually releasing a tiny bead.

Ivan was thrilled. "Oh, wow, that's amazing. What's it

made of?"

She peered at it, then smiled, "I don't believe it. I think you've found another artefact from the deep layer. It looks like a shell bead. We won't know until the lab has looked it over."

He was sure this was another sign from those people of long ago and felt a shiver run down his spine. He knew he would have to come here with Vlad soon to attempt to talk to these people.

As they walked back to the farmhouse, she told him about approaching the university. He shook his head, "I'm not clever enough to go there, and how can I study for exams, anyway."

Instead of arguing with him, she changed tack, "Tell me all about the stuff you've been reading. What have you learned?"

Now they were on a topic he felt happy to talk about to her. He explained about the different ways shamans worked, "When they go into this other state of consciousness, they travel to other worlds above or below and sometimes underwater to meet the spirits. They do this on behalf of individuals to identify how to heal physical, mental or emotional issues or discover what's wrong if there is a problem within the entire community."

She listened in silence, then replied, "You have quoted from all those books written by respected scientists. Although I don't go along with you, I cannot scoff at it either. But what you have just shown is how well you can study. Why not at least try for the exams? I'll get the books. You can carry on working as you are now and study at night. Just think, if you pass them, I could employ you to study for a bachelor's degree and work out here on the site. You'll earn much more than a shepherd, so your family will be better off too." She thought that would tip the balance.

He looked at her, shaking his head from side to side as if in denial, but the light in his eyes gave away his excitement. "Do you think I could do this?"

"Of course, you can, you're a smart kid, and this way, you can help your sisters much more."

He stood looking into the distance and thinking of all the possibilities. He could help his family, but more importantly, he could also help the spirits in the cave. Eventually, he nodded, "OK, I'll try it."

Soon he had the books, and everyone in the farmhouse knew he was studying for exams. He did not need to hide his books anymore. The visiting students were always happy to answer questions or show him where to find answers. The farmer's wife was so proud he was studying. Anyone would think he was her son. She made sure he had a table to work on, and sometimes when the kitchen was quiet, she would call him through to sit at the main table. Otherwise, she brought a little brazier into his room. Now it was an actual study room, no longer a small freezing bedroom as it had been when he started his learning journey, reading by the light of a candle while covered in blankets.

For the rest of the season, he went into the cave daily after all the workers had finished. He sat as the shaman book suggested but reserved the deeper trance-like states for his days off.

Both Ivan and Vlad had Sunday off, a rare occurrence. Which also meant the cave was quiet. They went to the site that night. They each had things to prepare, like a torch and blankets, and Vlad had to carry his drum. The shadows lengthened as they quietly left the farmhouse and picked up their luggage. They did not want to explain where they were going, much less what Ivan planned to do with the help of his friend.

Using their torches, they carefully picked their way to the very back of the cave and then down the gallery, which reached further back of the two. The one, the archaeologists, called the South Chamber. Ivan could not say why he wanted to be there, just that this spot felt right.

They spread the blankets, and Vlad made himself comfortable before starting his drumming while Ivan stretched out on the floor with his head close against the cave's back wall. The drumming softly continued. Vlad had been practising and could keep this up for quite some time. Ivan was more comfortable with the breathing patterns and closed his eyes. As daylight faded, they were in darkness. Vlad had his phone close in case he needed light.

Ivan went into his trance and saw a raised hill-like structure ahead of him with a massive hole in the centre. He felt a stab of fear. From the shamanic books, he was aware that was where he had to go. On approaching it, with no effort, he entered the aperture and immediately moved along a tunnel. Just like his first experience, the concentric circles remained circular until he came to an opening. As he stepped out, he saw he was in a vast cave; the ceiling was over twenty-foot above him. He looked around. He was in this cave, but long ago! He could see and know what was happening but could feel nothing. People were sitting around individual hearths, quietly talking. He watched as the children went to bed. He saw their beds were piles of bracken, covered with pelts. He continued to watch, and the adults also lay down. Soon there was silence in the cave. Then he saw them. Two men moved past him to the back of the cave and disappeared through the cave wall.

He wondered who they were. What were they doing? He had noticed these two before and speculated as to what they were doing.

Back in the cave long ago

Guta and his father entered their sacred cave. They had fasted all day. They had walked a long way, thinking and concentrating on the ritual they planned to do that night. It was only weeks until the Spring Burda. The tribal meeting held every two years.

Guta's father was the chief shaman and storyteller and had to take part in the business side of the meeting and the entertainment aspect with his stories. Guta, who had supported him for many years, knew it was time for the mantle of chief shaman/storyteller to pass onto his shoulders. For that, though, he needed a wife.

His father patted him on the shoulder, "We will speak to the spirits when we journey. We will ask for their help in procuring a wife for you."

As they passed quietly from their hearth close to the back of the cave, Ivan noticed a thin, dark fissure in the cave wall through which they entered. Ivan, as an invisible being, could follow them. They crept along slowly. It was a dark, tight squeeze of a passage that kinked a little. Then they had to go on all fours to crawl through a narrow hole before entering their "seeing" cave. It was so old no one knew who first discovered it. It was pitch dark here, but they both knew their way, and once in the sacred space, they set about making a small fire. Ivan settled well out of the way. It was strange to be here and yet not be here. He understood they intended this ritual as a seeing journey. That way, they would know if a wife was part of the spirits' plan. At other times they would come to talk to the spirits, to discover what ailed a person, and yet at different times to record important events in the shaman's life and the clan.

In the dim fire light, they sat with their eyes closed for a time as they chanted and clapped out the particular rhythms that would take them into the spirit's world, breathing shallowly and fast. Ivan copied them. As they saw pulsing lights flickering into zigzag lines followed by the strange sensations of floating, he was with them and terrified. As they experienced being pulled along a thread or thong, he observed their faces. For them, this was the most painful part of their journey. Strangely he also felt a strange sensation of being pulled, but no pain. He observed the spirits with their huge upside-down pear-shaped heads and big black, almond-shaped eyes who appeared to commune with the two shamans while Ivan remained an observer. He knew now that the spirits talking was not in words but more as if they heard things in their heads. It was always obscure and tortuous, so as shamans, they had to decipher it afterwards, and he was no wiser either.

Guta and his father were aware of a female presence, and from this, they concluded a wife was in the offing for Guta. They assumed the meeting of the woman destined to be his wife would occur at the Burda. Hours later, Ivan followed them as they silently returned to the main cave and sleep. As they went to their hearth, Ivan felt himself move through the tunnel again and arrive in his time. Once again, his body gave an involuntary shudder. He took a deep breath. His eyes opened into the blackness, with Vlad still tapping out the beat.

"You can stop that now, I'm back, but can you light the torch, please?"

Vlad scrambled to provide the torchlight. He had experienced terror and was pleased to have a light around them again. He did not want to linger there a moment longer and urged Ivan to go. They hastily packed up and made their way back to the farmhouse before Vlad would allow Ivan to speak at all, much less recount his experiences. Ivan was grateful as it gave him time to think since the experience also shook him. He became fascinated to think he watched shamans of old doing what he was learning. He knew this needed a lot of thought before talking about it to anyone.

On his next day off, Ivan paid a visit to his family. He knew his mother would understand his study of the shamanic books and what he had seen during the ritual. His father never spoke of any belief system. Still, his mother came from a tiny village, and they did not seem to have been so profoundly affected by the government decrees about religion, well, no religion.

Ivan knew she kept a little shrine in the drawer of her wardrobe. He had found it one day when he was very young and stirred things around, yelling, "Mumma look what I've found."

She hurried into the bedroom to see what he was doing. She snatched the tiny sprays of flowers and the little picture from him. She scolded him. "That is very naughty of you to look into other people's private places. Don't you dare do that again!"

He was shocked at her reaction; he had never opened her wardrobe again. Neither had she ever mentioned it. But he knew she was the right person to discuss his experiences in the shamanic state of consciousness.

A few days later, Sonja arrived to say they had identified the bead as coming from the deepest layer, "his" people, and they made it from an ostrich egg. Ivan grinned, remembering it had come from the extended galley area. Maybe it had even come from one of the men he had seen. It had been profoundly disturbing. Ivan was still not ready to discuss it with anyone, much less his friend Sonja. He knew he needed to share it with her, but only when it made sense in his head. He also knew he had to return and learn more about these men before discussing his experience with anyone.

Ivan and Vlad were not the only ones in the cave at

night. Days after their visit, a thin man dressed all in black parked his vehicle away from the farmhouse. He shaded his torch as he picked his way along the rough path and silently climbed the timber ramp into the cave. He stood as the original policeman had done, shone his torch into the cave roof, and slowly gazed at the walls and down to the floor. He could see where the workers had made trenches at the cave's far end as well as at the entrance. His lips twitched as he muttered to himself. "So Sonja, this is your new discovery. You wait until you see what I can do here. Soon it will be payback time." With a nasty grin, he made his way back to his car.

Chapter 4

A Story is Told

Ivan had to work hard at the new subjects, focusing on his latest books every evening until late. He was grateful for the lantern from Sonja and the brazier from the farmer's wife. Sometimes he despaired of ever grasping the topics. Maths was the most difficult until one of the archaeology students offered to help him. Instead of the dry examples in his textbook, his mentor changed them into everyday situations. Seen like that, Ivan grasped what had seemed perplexing puzzles. He could practice their use again in daily activities until he thoroughly understood the concepts. This pleased him so much that he felt he deserved an evening off.

"Vlad, would you like to come to the cave for another drumming session?"

"Ivan, I'd love to, but I promised to take Tanya out this evening. Would tomorrow be ok for you? I could come over after work."

Ivan smiled. This Tanya was Vlad's girlfriend. She was the daughter of one of the farm workers. They had been sweethearts since school days, although, unlike Vlad, she had been able to go on with her education but had no intention of moving away from home. She had a job at the local dairy.

The next evening as they walked to the cave, Ivan said, "I read in the shaman book we need to use the drum because it causes changes in the brain."

Vlad looked happy, "Does that mean the more I play it, the cleverer I'll get?"

"No, don't be such an idiot, it can't change how stupid or clever you are, but it helps the shaman to travel to the unfamiliar spirit worlds. Our shamans who live in far north of Siberia call their drums their horse."

Vlad looked crestfallen, "So what do I get out of this playing?"

"You get to being the donkey that makes the horse work!"

By now, they had reached the site and carefully stepped past the scaffolding and the deep trenches branching like blood vessels in every direction. A missed step and a fall into a trench could cause a serious injury. They reached the same spot as before, right at the back where excavations had not started. They made themselves comfortable, and then Ivan lay down, closed his eyes, and lifted a hand. Vlad knew to start his drumming. Slowly Ivan was aware of strange flickering shapes behind his eyelids. He concentrated on them as they took on more definite forms. At first, Ivan thought of it as cross-hatching, longish lines going down and shorter, going across, making lots of shapes like ladders.

All the while, he continued to breathe deeply and slowly. As he watched, they slowly melted away and became curved lines like tiny boats. Curves eventually covered these over too. Then he noticed he was moving along a different tunnel this time, one without the concentric rings, more like steep sides of a cliff that leaned in so he could not see any sky. He allowed himself to wonder where he was going. Then suddenly, he burst out into a strange place. There were mountains all around. Directly ahead were two peaks with a curve of land between them, the same shaped curve he had seen earlier when he moved into his trance. Now, in front of him was a massive flat area with bright green grass. He could see a stream of crystal clear water tumbling beside him, which he knew was icy cold. He saw it flow into a lake, only a small one, but deep and still. He walked on a little further and saw tepee-like tents spreading out in circles around him. The inhabitants constructed the tent walls of dried skins stretched over a cone-like tree pole structure. The thought came to him that these people must have hauled these poles here as there was no sign of trees for miles around. Then he saw a small herd of horses quietly eating the grass at the far end of the lake. He watched as there seemed to be many people coming and going. He wondered what they were doing. It looked like a meeting place. As he stood staring at people hurrying around him, he realised they could not see him again. He strode around, looking at the tents and all the people dressed in fancy tunics made of cured animal skins with matching leggings. The women wore their tunics long to mid-calf, while the men had shorter ones with leggings. He noticed a youthful woman with a stunning tunic decorated with fringes across the front, and on the ends were little white beads! He had seen one like that not so long before.

That thought brought him back to the cave, but still in the time of "his" people. It must have been early spring, and he could see distinct areas of activity this time. Near the front, on his left, was a group of people tapping rocks. He knew they were the knappers. The excavations had already found evidence of their activity. Close to them was a striking woman with ebony hair and dark brown eyes, unlike those around her who had brownish hair and were blue-eyed. She was busy with her hands. It looked as if she was making something from grasses. Then he saw the young shaman he had watched in the secret cave. He immediately felt a bond with him. As Ivan stood to the side of the cave, he saw the shaman was talking to the people. Ivan understood the shaman was also the storyteller, and that's why people were waiting. They had eaten their meal and now wanted entertainment.

Ivan watched as the flickering firelight lit up the faces of the clan, and Guta asked, "What story would you like to hear tonight?"

The raspy voice of an old lady piped up, "Tell us about when you met Kitam."

Those sitting around the fire nodded their agreement. It had been a good day hunting. Now everyone was replete and happy to sit contentedly digesting their meal and being entertained hearing the oft-told story.

Guta sat cross-legged and smiled. Rocking back and forth, he began his tale. "Long ago, an engaging young man went to the Burda with his parents. As his father was the chief shaman/storyteller, they had to get there early. His father kept him busy on their first day, but by the evening, one clan arrived late. Since it was after dark, he, along with many other younger men, ran over to help the tired people set up their sleeping shelters while the women hastily stirred up their fires and threw more food into the cooking containers. Along with the other youths busy tying the poles and flinging skins over to make the shelters, Guta turned around and saw a beautiful maiden coming toward them.

As he looked at her, the noise of the camp died away. He could see nothing but this person approaching them. His best friend dug him in the ribs and told him to get on with his job and stop staring, but she entranced Guta. She smiled at them and asked for help as one of the hut poles that also formed the sledge had fallen off the horse. Now both sledge and pole were stuck fast, she could not move either, and the horse had gone off to join its fellows. Guta shoved the others away and hurried off to help her.

For the rest of the Burda, whenever Guta was free, they could find him near this beautiful girl. They talked, laughed, and danced with all the others, but it was as if they were alone. His father spoke to him at least once, but it was like the wind blowing. The lad was there doing all his physical jobs, but his mind was not there. His father decided the situation needed sorting. He sent for the girl's father. They talked long into the night and agreed they could marry the two young people by the next Burda. Then she would return with Guta to his clan cave.

At the end of the Burda meeting, all the people returned to their home caves, the man full of dreams. He knew he had until the next Burda, only two springs away, to prepare for one of the most significant steps in his life."

He reminded his listeners that as it was clan tradition, the shaman/storyteller did not have to hunt but received a portion of their kill. In times of plenty, this was good, but if the hunt had gone badly, this put a strain on everyone. They all nodded at this and smiled as he continued, "My father insisted whenever we went out to discuss our work on matters of ritual or a new story, we should always take our bows and arrows. We were shamans, not hunters, so we did not take a spear. But we could often catch small meat like rabbit or fowl for our food. As a result, I had rabbit pelts and feathers to swap for hides with you hunters."

His audience nodded. They knew this and agreed this was a fair way of working. Guta went on, "My mother could make me a tunic ready for the big day", and looking around at his audience, he smiled, "While your wives had soft rabbit skins to wrap your babies."

"Before we left for the next Burda, I prepared a hearth

next door to my parents. It made me think when I came back, there would be two of us here."

His audience smiled, knowing that is how they had felt when they, too, had made that big emotional and mental step, yet for most of them, it was a small physical one. All except the ones who had moved into this cave clan as Kitam had on her marriage.

He continued, "Getting ready to leave for the next Burda, I thought everyone was so slow and the journey, well, I am sure it took us twice as long, as usual, to get there."

A member of the audience called out, "No, you made such a fuss. We had to hurry all the time. I think it took us less time than ever before or since."

Everyone laughed, "Go on with the story!"

Guta did as he was told, "As we walked down the path between the cliffs, my heart was pounding, I wanted to yell out that soon I would see Kitam again, but my Mother scowled at me and shook her head. She showed that it was not the right behaviour for the son of the chief shaman/storyteller. Having crossed the pass, we came out on the grass at the base of the cliffs beside the tinkling, crystal-clear water. The lake was shining and still as ever, but not so my heart. I looked around. My heart fell. I wanted to sink to the ground and cry. My father scowled and said we had to set up the shelters. As the chief storyteller, my father needed to be at the meeting place a day or so earlier than the rest of the tribe to give him time to prepare. One of the smaller clans hurried over to greet us and help to get things ready. They had a very long way to come and also tried to be there early to give themselves time to rest before the crucial part of the tribe arrived."

The central camp was ready. The communal fire was lit, but still no Kitam and family. By now, my heart was breaking. Maybe they had decided not to come this year. Perhaps they had decided they wanted their daughter to stay close to them. She might even have changed her mind. I could not sleep that night. I decided if they did not come or send word by the end of the Burda, I would leap into the judgment pool where we plunge people who have committed terrible crimes to their deaths."

His listeners shook their heads. They wondered how anyone could contemplate such a terrible act.

He let them experience his profound feelings of rejection and the terrible consequences. "The next day, my father swamped me with work carrying messages all over the place. I kept glancing over to the end of the path from the cliffs where the path opens out, watching to see who the recent arrivals were. They trickled in all day, but there was no Kitam. My mother needed more water, so she sent me off to the stream on the other side of the lake to collect a bag full. As I walked back, my eyes strayed to the path yet again. This time it rewarded me as I saw Kitam and her family, tired and plodding onto the grass. I dropped the water bag and rushed over to them. I looked at this beautiful girl and forgot all the words I wanted to say. Instead, I stood there looking and grinning."

One of the audience called out, "I remember your mother was furious with you for not bringing the water. I had to get some for her. You should have heard her grumbling!"

Guta nodded, "Yes, I remember, and Kitam laughed at me. For once, I had no words."

They all looked at each other and nodded in agreement. That year it was a very productive meeting. Besides Guta and Kitam's wedding, two other couples wed, and one girl from this clan went to be a hunter's wife in another cave.

Guta continued, "I was so busy at the Burda we hardly had time to talk, but on the way back, I remember talking so much I forgot to show Kitam the safe pathway through the water and sinking sands. Much later, as we came up the steep path, we heard a shout from those who had stayed behind. A crowd of you rushed down to meet us weary travellers and horses and help carry our heavy burdens up the slope. The welcome you gave my recently married wife was wonderful. She was shy but expected a positive outcome to the negotiations. She had brought with her a little gift for each family of her new clan, a clever plan, you must agree. I recall seeing so many of you waving and calling as we walked up the path. The welcome feast was the best we have ever had."

An old man butted in, "It was no different to any other one; it's just you were different. It happens to all of us." He tipped his head to the side, "Well, maybe not quite all of us."

Everyone laughed. They knew he had married a shrewish little woman who had made his life miserable, always complaining about his hunting skills, which were pretty rudimentary since he was one of their best knappers. Two winters ago, in the dark, cold time, she had fallen ill and died, much to his relief and the surrounding hearths.

After a few moments, Guta continued, "That shy woman soon made friends with all of you, and that is how Kitam came to this cave."

When he finished talking, he sat gazing into space, remembering that beautiful woman. She stood at the entrance wearing the greenstone bracelet with its bead dangling over her wrist. Other than her, he had seen nothing so beautiful. It fitted perfectly around her slim, elegant wrist. It had been a wedding gift from her parents. He noticed apart from special occasions, she did not wear it and supposed it was too fragile to withstand the wear and tear of their everyday lives.

Ivan experienced a sense of achievement, having participated in this episode in the lives of the people of old. He understood the first site he had visited must be the Burda. Without control or direction, he felt sucked along the tunnel and spat out into his everyday body. Slowly he opened his eyes and spoke to Vlad, who quickly lit the torch.

Vlad was shaking, "Are you all right? You seemed to thrash around a bit now and again, and you called out once. I was unsure if I should summon you with the four sharp beats again."

"I'm glad you didn't. That was amazing. I travelled to a strange place where these people went for meetings, and then I came back here and listened to the shaman tell a story. I now know his name is Guta, don't ask me how I know. I just do."

"Well, whatever, we better be getting back to the farmhouse, it's late, and we both have to work tomorrow."

In silence, they walked back to the farmhouse. Later, Ivan made notes about his evening journeys. He knew when he told Sonja about these adventures, she would want to know practical things, one of which he realised was the site of this Burda or meeting place.

Sonja's vehicle rattled into the farmyard. It was early. Ivan was only getting his sheep ready to go out for the day. He looked over and grinned. "You're here early. Couldn't you sleep?"

She smiled at her protegee. "Of course, I can sleep, but I wanted to catch you before you disappear into Siberia's wilds with your faithful flock."

He was pleased as he wanted to tell her about the journey last night. "As you have your boots on, why not walk awhile with me? We can talk while the family eat."

She grabbed a notebook and bag from the truck, and they set off.

She said, "I'm intrigued. What do you want to tell me?"

"Vlad and I went into the cave last night for him to drum and me to travel in a trance. It is getting easier, and sometimes I have a little control but not this time."

She stopped and looked quizzically at him. "Go on. I'm interested."

"Well, I turned up at their Burda. A narrow cliff path leads down to a wide-open area beside a lake. On the opposite side of the lake, there are twin peaks with a strange curved spine between them. All this should still be identifiable even after all these years."

Now she was excited. "Right, we need maps of the whole area in as much detail as possible. You're right. Physical features should remain similar so we can find them on a map, especially if they are as distinctive as you describe them. Do you say they travel with horses and their equipment?" She looked thoughtful for a moment. " That means it must be quite a distance from this cave. Do you have any idea how long they travelled?"

He shook his head, sorry he could not measure time on these otherworld travels.

Chapter 5

Life and Death

Ivan had a short journey into their world on one of his journeys to visit "his" people. He spent a long time observing them as Vlad obligingly drummed away. By now, he, too, could drift into a strange space. Not a trance but leaving behind all the worries and responsibilities of his ordinary life.

After visiting so often, Ivan could recognise the main characters within the cave, especially Guta and his wife, Kitam. As he watched, he noticed the layout of the cave. Each family had a specially designated area. Ivan called them hearths in his mind as they made up each person's home space. For him, it made sense the ones at the back of the cave were for higher-status individuals, like the shaman and Een, the clan leader who was also their best hunter. It would be warmer in the bitter winter months away from the draughts, which could still sneak around the sides of the Auroch curtain. In the middle of the cave were a central fireplace and an open area around it. Ivan presumed it was for communal activities or listening to stories. Right at the front of the cave on the left-hand side was an area set aside for the horses. They came and went at will. Usually, the mares with tiny foals would shelter out from the worst of the swirling snowstorms. The humans welcomed their presence as it was an added source of warmth. After it dried, the humans used horse dung to fuel the fires.

Een got on well with Guta's family, especially after he met another hunter not of their tribe, Aiee. She was slim, with dark skin and brown eyes, and her long straight black hair was always pulled tightly back off her face and coiled into a knot held with an ivory pin. Blessed with excellent eyesight, she was formidable with her bow and arrows. Sadly seven years after her marriage, she was injured fighting a cave bear. The great beast had taken a swipe at her, it should have killed her, but instead, she tumbled down a slope and unfortunately broke her leg. The other hunters had distracted the bear and finally killed it, which saved her life but not her lifestyle. Her leg had not healed straight, leaving her lame and unable to hunt. Undeterred, she took up an essential task, basket weaving. In no time, she became the best at the close-woven basket bowls. The grasses and the weave made them waterproof, so everyone used them for heating water and cooking. Since her living space at the back of the cave was dark, she worked towards the front of the cave. Near the knapping area, it allowed her to watch all the activities of the clan swirling around her.

After Guta married, he arranged the hearths so Kitam had a cooking place of her own next to his parents. Their little hide shelter afforded them privacy. Soon she was accepted and absorbed into the everyday life of the clan, and as time went on, she proved herself an able, hard-working member of the community.

Their old medicine woman quickly discovered this newcomer had extensive knowledge of herbs and their medicinal uses. She made Kitam her acolyte, who was already proficient in many respects. The old lady decided she would teach this young woman everything she knew, and soon they were good friends. As the older woman was childless and a widow, she became part of their family by living at their hearth in her little shelter tent.

Poor Guta, because of his separate hearth, knew he must hunt like the other men to provide for his family. However, as the son of the Shamen/storyteller, he also had to attend rites and rituals with his father, which meant going on vision quests to help heal an individual of ailments beyond the scope of the medicine woman's talents or solve problems more extensive issues. The others would gladly provide food for the little group on these occasions. Fortunately, Kitam soon proved to be very resourceful at setting traps to catch small animals, which bolstered the family fare besides the few Guta could get with his bow and arrows.

In time Kitam fell pregnant, and Guta was overjoyed. Everything progressed as usual until a few weeks before she was due. Then disaster struck, and she started bleeding. The old medicine woman could not stop it. After many hours Kitam gave birth to twins. Sadly the smallest, the boy, never breathed. The medicine woman was more interested in saving the mother's life. Guta was beside himself with grief at the loss of the baby boy and having to find another clan member to be a wet nurse for the little girl. He was frantic about the real possibility of losing his beloved Kitam.

He left the girl child with a wet nurse. During her pregnancy, this poor woman lost her husband in a freak hunting accident. Then her baby was stillborn. The delight of being given this baby girl was immeasurable. Soon she behaved as if she was her child. It was as if the spirits had given her another chance at motherhood.

The young woman, Kitam, lay still and pale for days. The medicine woman stewed mixtures of leaves and bark and dribbled some onto the lips of the girl, a few drops got into her mouth, and the swallowing reflex ensured she had some medicine. All the clan came to stand at the entrance to the hearth. They offered their condolences for the loss of the baby boy. They gazed at the still form of the mother. They were sure she, too, would be joining her babe. Guta sat beside her for hours, holding her hand and telling her she still had work to do here; she must not go to the spirit world yet.

At last, his Father called Guta over, "The only way we can save your wife is to do a ritual for the baby and bring your wife's power back from the shadowlands."

Ivan watched the sad proceedings. He experienced a shadow of the emotional turmoil of Guta at the loss of their longed-for son. Ivan sympathised with Guta's anxiety about Kitam. He wondered as the medicine woman washed the tiny body before handing it to the two shamans. Gently they rubbed the frail little body with precious red ochre and wrapped him in a soft covering of rabbit skin but not before Guta had placed a tiny green stone bead in his son's hand. They then covered the furry bundle with a thick hide and walked out of the cave.

As they walked, Ivan could follow. They journeyed for some time until they came to a low hillock. Ivan noted the area, knowing he would need to find this place again. He observed them hauling brambles aside to reveal a low entrance to a small cave. From the confident way Guta had led his Father, it was apparent only he knew of the existence of this cave. They scrambled in, pulling the rawhide bundle behind them. The soil in the cave was soft, unlike outside, which was still hard from the frozen winter. Crouching all the time, they were able to dig a deep grave. Ivan wondered why a grave as he had seen these people place their dead on what he called in his mind the "death rock." He also knew they then brought the bones back into the cave. Why this departure? Then he figured Guta wanted to ensure no animal could scavenge and disturb his tiny son's sleep. He watched as they walked silently back to the home cave. Still not speaking, they reached the rear, moving along the dark passage to their sacred space. Ivan followed them in and sat out of the way, watching but able to experience Guta's fear for Kitam and the heartache at the loss of his son.

They lit a fire, sprinkling dried herbs into the flames this time. Soon the area was swirling with aromatic smoke. Their rhythmic clapping and singing, which they could perform automatically, took them to the place they called the land of the spirits. Ivan realised only people with the same neurological wiring as him, modern humans, could only experience these feelings. Leading him to accept that although they were so far back in history as to be termed prehistory, their neurological makeup was no different to him. This information made him feel even closer to them and more determined to discover as much as possible about them.

As he observed the two shamans moving into their altered states of consciousness, he learned the older man was busy singing to the spirits, telling them of the new arrival and asking them to accept him into their world. The tempo changed as the two sang in unison, begging the spirits to let go of Kitam and allow her to return.

After reading about shamanic belief, Ivan recognised they had travelled to the lower world, searching for the missing part of Kitam's soul. Seeing a spirit otter in three poses indicated the spirits had granted their request. Holding the spirit animal close to his body Guta and his father returned to their earth plane. Exhausted and dripping with sweat, Guta held tightly to the spirit animal. Guta's Father lit a torch, and they sat for a while until their rapidly beating hearts had returned to their usual rhythm, their breathing again slow and steady. Then it was time to make the dark journey back to the life of the cave. They carefully approached Kitam. The medicine woman nodded, knowing they had returned with the magic necessary to heal Kitam.

Guta blew through his hands onto her chest as the medicine woman watched and nodded her head in approval. The spirit animal, Kitam's guardian spirit, was back with her. She should recover soon. Ivan watched them stepping back and gazing down at the still woman. As he watched the little group, it amazed him as her eyes slowly flickered before opening. She looked at Guta, her beautiful eyes bright and seeing again. She had returned from the dead, but she was fragile.

Her mother-in-law, the old medicine woman, and Aiee took turns caring for her. Ivan knew that by slowly sipping the broth they gave her, Kitam regained her strength. But the medicine woman said she doubted Kitam would have any more babies. The old woman and Guta agreed not to tell Kitam about the living child as the foster mother was due to get married again and move to another cave. Guta was happy to let the child go as the price for restoring his beloved wife. That was all that mattered, although he knew she would be unhappy knowing she could not have another child.

At the next Burda, Kitam told her mother about losing the baby. It saddened her mother at the loss of a grandchild. She reassured her daughter there was always time for others and not to worry. Kitam did not want to tell her the truth. There would be no more children. Instead, she threw herself into all the aspects of training as a medicine woman. While at the Burda, she exchanged some rabbit pelts for herbs. Ones she knew grew neither near the cave nor in the area they travelled through each summer and autumn.

Life was difficult, but she appreciated it was not as bad as poor Aiee. The two had grown close over the time they were neighbours. Aiee had pain most of the time, yet her lovely smile would fool most of the clan except Kitam and the old medicine woman. They offered her herbs to help with the pain, but being stubborn, Aiee shook her head. She preferred the pain and a clear head. When they journeyed to their summer camp, it was different. The walking was both painful and challenging. Then she welcomed their medicine and accepted she would have to ride. Een ensured a spare horse was in the baggage train for that eventuality. She also had to ride on the rare occasions she travelled with the clan to the Burda. However, Aiee volunteered to remain and look after the old and those not healthy enough to make the long trip. Kitam was very grateful for being able to leave a stash of herbal medicines with someone so sensible when she had to go as the wife of the shaman.

Watching the drama of birth in the lives of these "his people" made Ivan think more about his parents and their struggle to look after four children. He also appreciated how much they had sacrificed for their children.

Ivan and Bone set off to visit his parents. Since this last spirit encounter, he viewed his family differently. After getting off the bus, the ram and the young man walked along the rough stone track to his family home. Once the greetings were over, Ivan explained about Bone.

"Dad, this sheep caused me to find the cave. My employer says I can keep him, but he must not go near the ewes. That isn't easy now he is fully grown. I don't want him killed, so I wondered if I could leave him with you. Maybe we could get a couple of ewes, and you would have the beginning of a new way of life."

His dad had a faraway look in his eyes, "You know, my son, that is a great idea. I can charge a stud fee for this fine ram covering the local ewes. Then as you say, buy in a couple of ewes of our own." Turning to his wife, "Mum, we could even milk them. Should they have males, we could slaughter them and have a bit of meat during the winter. The females we can get covered by another ram and slowly grow a flock of our own."

His three sisters crowded around Ivan, demanding to know all about the goings-on in the cave. By now, they, like all their neighbours, knew about Ivan's part in the cave's discovery. The girls were thrilled that the real cause of all the fuss, the ram, was coming to live with them. Bone seemed to know this was his new home and wandered off to find a quick bite. When Ivan left that evening, Bone was safely ensconced in the little lean-to abutting the wall where the chimney was so he was warm and snug. Ivan felt lost without his friend but knew it was for the best for Bone and Ivan's family.

Chapter 6

Testing Time

Spring nearly a year later

As he went into the farmhouse at the end of the day a few weeks before he was due to write his exams, the farmer's wife handed him a letter. She said, "Ivan, this came to the house today. It doesn't have your name, but we think it must be for you as it's addressed to The Person who Found the Bone in the Cave. My husband doesn't like the look of it, but we thought you better open it and see what they say."

Ivan took it and went off to his room. He preferred the privacy of reading anything rather than a free for all in the kitchen. Sitting at his desk surrounded by study books, he opened it and read.

I am from the University and need to check if the work in the cave is being done to the highest standards. There is no need for you to inform Dr Sokalov. I will send someone to meet you at the cave entrance after all the workers have left tomorrow evening.

The letter gave Ivan a fluttering sensation in his stomach. On his return to the kitchen, the farmer's wife glanced up from serving the food. "Are you alright, Ivan? You look odd."

He swallowed. "Um, yes, it's alright."

He left early the following morning before anyone could question him, but he felt a tightening in his stomach and was visibly sweating.

At the end of that day, after everyone had trailed up the muddy path, Ivan made his way to the entrance, still feeling uncomfortable. He stood looking around, but there was no one there. He was turning to leave when a voice rang out. "Not so quick, bone finder."

Ivan spun round as a hairy arm stopped him as it curled about his neck. In a panic, Ivan jerked and jabbed his elbow into his attacker's stomach. The grip slackened slightly, which gave Ivan time to turn and face his attacker. They grappled, staggering to and fro, and then the attacker stumbled and went over on his ankle. He held tight onto his opponent, but Ivan pushed him away. His opponent swayed back and forward before falling into the trench. A moment later, an unearthly screech rose from the depths. Ivan peered over the edge. The man lay on his back, his leg at a strange angle. Now he kept bellowing. "Get help."

Ivan decided the best thing was to do just that. He ran into the kitchen. "Quick, I need help. Call the police and an ambulance."

A crowd of workers went down to see what was needed.

Soon a spotlight was rigged, and a first aider knelt beside the injured man. They covered him with a blanket. At the same time, the workers lowered a ramp to be able to move the patient.

After the paramedics had him on a trolley and loaded him into the ambulance, the police questioned Ivan.

It was the policeman who had questioned Ivan when he found the bone. He still looked angry. "How come you were fighting in such a dangerous place?"

Ivan said, "I wasn't fighting. As per the letter, I went down to the cave, and a great hairy guy attacked me."

"What letter? Bring it to me."

As his exams drew nearer, Ivan felt anxious for the first time. However, the students helping him were sure he would do fine. Without warning, they questioned Ivan whenever he was at the farmhouse. All the students were keen for him to succeed and asked poor Ivan questions on many topics every time they saw him. Most of the time, the answers were correct. They declared he was ready to sit his exams.

The police confirmed the man injured in the fall into the trench was there to, as he said, "Rough up the boy so he wouldn't be able to do his examinations."

He was a gang member, and the leader gave him his orders. He had no idea who they came from in the first place.

Sonja arrived close to the appointed day to give him a ride into the city.

On the way there, she spoke, "I hope you don't mind, but I've arranged for you to stay with my parents this weekend and the days of the exams. I live in a tiny studio flat. They have a house, and my father has a car. Since he's a senior professor in the Humanities Department, he goes in every day and will give you a lift to the University for your exams."

Ivan looked a trifle anxious hearing this news. But she laughed and said, "Don't worry, they won't eat you. My mother has organised a dinner party on Saturday night, which gives you Sunday to recover before your exams start on Monday. She loves entertaining and always has a few interesting people for dinner. I'm sure you'll enjoy everybody's company."

"But I haven't got smart clothes to wear to dinner."

She patted his arm, "Don't worry. We're going to solve that problem. Here's the departmental store where they'll have everything you need. Don't worry about the cost because I've got an account here. It's my way of thanking you for finding the cave and exciting prospects."

When they arrived at Sonja's family home, it surprised him that it was a modest-sized house. Her parents were waiting at the door to greet and conduct him into their little world. The hall had a series of paintings. Ivan looked and shook his head. The main subject was buildings he gathered from all around the world. With a tinge of pride, Sophia, Sonja's mum, said, "They are all buildings I have designed. Most of them incorporate unusual features. I try to make them blend in with the surroundings and use echo-based features. His eyes were wide as he looked at them. One seemed to be a hanging garden. Another appeared to have trees growing from it. Most intriguing was a photo of humps in a desert. He looked closely, and Maxime smiled, wondering if the young man knew what he saw. He said, "That's one of Sophia's triumphs. Ivan thought it could not be too much of a challenge to make humps in a desert. Maxime laughed. "You don't know what you are looking at, do you?"

Ivan shrugged and said, "No, they look like humps of desert sand."

"No, look closer. See those lighter-coloured threads? They are roads."

"So, why does a road lead to a sand dump?"

Maxime said, "You need to see the 3D version. Come into the lounge."

The lounge had bookshelves, some with books but many with strange objects. Ivan blinked as he looked about. It felt as if he had strayed into Aladdin's cave. Maxime beckoned

Ivan to a small table with a model of the humps. Still none the wiser, Maxime lifted the covering. There was a rambling house with rooms and passages going in all directions.

Ivan took a step back with a slow, disbelieving shake of his head. "That's incredible. How does it work?"

The units are all pre-formed shells fixed to a concrete base. Each one is bolted to the next. When all the utilities are in place, and the house is ready, it is covered, depending on the surroundings. Here with desert sand but at other sites in turf or, I guess, even snow."

"Now you see why she is highly thought of in her profession. When she is not breaking boundaries, she teaches at the university."

Maxime Sokolov continued, "It's such a pleasure to meet you. Sonja has spoken of you often and feels you have great archaeological potential. But I wanted to hear from you. How do you feel about studying? Where do you feel it will take you?"

After this unusual introduction to the family home, Ivan felt comfortable talking to this gentleman. Although they had only known each other for a few minutes, he felt safe to talk about some challenges he had experienced with his studying. "Well, ever since I found that bone, I feel a close connection to those early people. The students at the dig have been brilliant, helping me with my studies and, more recently, testing me at every opportunity. I feel I owe it to Sonja, the students, and most of all, to those ancient people. I want to pass these exams and go on to study archaeology.

Sonja poked her head around the door, "Come, Ivan, let me show you to your room, you can unpack, and then we'll have a meal."

She showed him along a passage to a beautiful big room, "This has always been the spare room. For some strange reason, my parents felt I did not need much space, so my room was up in the attic. My flat is not much bigger, but I like the sense of freedom it gives me. In case you feel lost, I'll spend the weekend here too. You needn't feel deserted."

He unpacked his lovely new clothes, two pairs of jeans and a decent pair of trousers, a few T-shirts and a smart shirt for Saturday evening. She had even seen to it that he had bought a new pair of shoes and a pair of comfortable sneakers. He had never had so much and especially new clothes. He washed his hands and face, combed his hair, put on a new T-shirt and was ready to go downstairs again. Over dinner, the conversation flowed over many topics, which fascinated Ivan, just hearing what they thought and did. He did not participate very much until Sonja's mother asked, "So Ivan tell us all about your discovery of the cave."

He squirmed in his seat and went red with embarrassment. He took a deep breath and started. He talked about the lamb and why it went into the cave. His surprise at finding a bone. His terror of the policeman. He told them how Bone had grown into a handsome ram he had taken to his parents. He told them about his father, hoping Bone could be the start of a business.

They had driven in from the farm, and after all these new experiences, Sonja could see Ivan was tired. "Ivan, I think you have talked enough and seen enough for the day. Why don't you take yourself off to bed? We're going to do some exploring tomorrow."

Sophia said, "You can explore all you like but make sure you are home in time for our dinner party."

As usual, Ivan was up early the following day. The place was silent, the garden birds were singing at the top of their throats, but he could not hear any activity in the house. He washed and dressed to be ready to participate in whatever Sonja had organised for the day. For him, it turned out to be a day of exploration. First, she took him to the museum. She wanted to show him the exhibits from other archaeological explorations and historical ones so he could absorb the enormity of time where the people of the cave fit into the timeline.

They went on to the zoo. They gazed at the animals. "Sonja, I think I like all the big cats best. They are so graceful but with pent-up energy. You feel the latent danger just looking at them, don't you?"

Finally, she took him up to see her office at the University. He said something as they walked along the corridor, and she laughed. She saw someone, and the relaxed look on her face vanished. A short, thin man dressed in a black top and trousers stood outside a door a little further along. He glowered at them as she went to open her door. "Good afternoon Yagor. What are you doing here on a Saturday afternoon?"

He sneered, "I could ask the same thing of you. So this is the wonder boy who pushes people into trenches. I presume now he is your toy boy. I've heard about you and your father conniving to get him into the University. I suppose your father is so desperate with you being unmarried he'll help you grab anyone but a kid like this? "

Sonja looked stunned, then swung around and hastily opened her door. "Come on in, Ivan. Please excuse that vulgar little man."

Ivan saw she was close to tears. "What's going on? Is my being here a problem for you or your father?"

She grabbed a tissue and dabbed at her eyes. "No, you're not a problem. That is one of the lecturers, Yegor Morozov. He's a nasty, mean-minded man with a mind like a sewer. I fully understand why his wife left him. We both applied for this job, head of the Archaeology Department and I was appointed. He has never forgiven me and is always unpleasant. Come to think of it, how did he know of the trench incident? I'm wondering if we have a security breach. No one has said anything about it until we know who employed him."

Ivan slumped into the easy chair as Sonja sat at her desk. His sense of elation after the morning experiences was now a distant memory. He looked concerned as Sonja tried to pull herself together. "What did he mean calling me a toy boy? It didn't sound as if it was something nice. I'm not a boy anyway." Ivan sat and looked about the office thoughtfully. "I'll remember to stay away from him if I'm lucky enough to get accepted."

Sonja sniffed hard, took a deep breath and said, "Come, let me show you the exam venue."

Ivan looked at the room. "It's not too big. I thought it would be huge. But I don't mind telling you I'm scared. More than when I found the bone and had to speak to the policeman."

Sonja laughed. "I've heard good things about your studying from the other students. Of course, you are scared, but I am sure you'll be fine. We better get back before my mother gets angry with us for being late. Anyway, I have to help with some preparations."

Back at the house, he felt butterflies in his tummy at the prospect of a dinner party. Not even his new clothes were able to lift his mood. His greatest fear was making a fool of himself in front of the guests and embarrassing Sonja. He glanced at the mirror to see himself in the new clothing. He acknowledged they looked good. He stood up straighter and said to his image. "Smile at everyone. Only speak when you are spoken to and listen to what the others are saying." He hoped he could move into this way of life with the same ease as putting on his new outfit. He was sure the evening would demonstrate if he could make a future in this academic world that Sonja offered.

The front door opened, and the first guest entered. When Ivan saw Mikhail, relief flooded through him. He called, "Hello, Mikhail. I'm so glad to see you are one of the guests. At least there will be one person I know. I expect the other will be a typical academic."

The petite woman standing behind Mikhail stuck her head around him and said, "Be careful what you say, young man."

Ivan went red in the face and stammered. "I'm so sorry I didn't see you there."

Her laugh was like a donkey braying. "Nobody sees me behind my husband but make no mistake where the power emanates!"

Sonja arrived and said, "Ah, I see you've met."

The other woman looked him over and said, "No, I presume this is the prodigy, Ivan."

Sonja smiled. "Ivan, this is Zoya. She's Mikhail's wife."

Soon they were all seated at the table, and there was a buzz of conversation. Zoya tossed her mop of curly black hair as she laughed. "Well, Ivan, which of us would you say was the typical academic?"

He was saved from finding an answer but politely said, "I know Mikhail is a paleo-anthropologist. I think I know what that entails but what is your speciality?"

When she said, "I'm a Palio ontologist." Ivan's face fell. He didn't have a clue what that was. Sonja saw him struggling and said, "Zoya studies life before and sometimes including what we now call the ice ages. She examines fossils to determine their interaction with each other. As well as their contribution to how modern humans evolved."

Now Ivan experienced a sense of sameness with both husband and wife.

Although Ivan did not drink, the others enjoyed their wine except Sonja, who preferred vodka. Soon the buzz of conversation drowned out any fears Ivan had of being in such distinguished company. Sonja observed his shoulders relax and was pleased he offered the occasional observation. Sonja looked over at her mother, and they exchanged a look which said more than words. They were both sure he would fit in with their tight-knit group.

Mikhail said, "You asked if shamanism is about spirit communication. How are you progressing with your shamanic work?"

Ivan regaled them about some of his experiences. Suddenly, Zoya tapped on her husband's arm. "Tell him about Korgai."

Mikhail scowled, "Yes, alright. I was planning to get to it just now."

After the meal, they all helped clear up and wash the dishes. Sophia and Maxime had never seen the need for things like dishwashers. Once settled and drinking coffee in the lounge, they asked Ivan about his study preparation for these exams.

Mikhail smiled, cleared his throat and said, "Here is a carrot to get you through the exams. A friend of mine is the leading shaman in northern Siberia, well, to be precise, in the Arctic area, as they don't bother about the borders like down here." He looked at Sonja, eyebrows raised. "Would you object if I invited him to visit the cave and Ivan?"

Sonja grinned but said, "I think it's time I told all of you something. Someone lured Ivan to the cave site by saying they needed to inspect the work for the University. When Ivan arrived, no one was there until he turned to go. Then a guy, who had been lurking in the shadows, leapt out and attacked Ivan. There was a struggle; fortunately, the right guy fell in a trench and broke his leg."

Sophia looked horrified. "What if they attacked you, Sonja?"

Mikhail said, "It's my guess it was to prevent Ivan from coming here to write these exams. It makes me think it might have something to do with that rat Yegor."

Sonja's eyes flew wide. "I'd never even considered him, but he did make a strange comment when we bumped into him this afternoon outside my office."

Mikhail snorted. "What was he doing there on a Saturday?"

Sonja looked thoughtful. "You know the whole interaction was bizarre. He was his usual rude self. Then he commented about a trench. To be honest, I was upset as he said some unpleasant things ending with Ivan being a toy boy. By then, I retreated into my office in tears."

Maxime had been following the conversation, then broke in. "If you have any more trouble with him, let me know. I'll report him to the governors and see he is duly reprimanded."

Sonja shook her head. "Thanks, Dad, but I can fight my own battles."

Zoya was sensitive to the rising tensions and turned to Ivan. "Tell me more about the shamanic work you are learning."

Ivan recognised her ploy and described some of his journeys and encounters with the people of the deeper layers of the cave. The people who he now considered and thought of as "his" people. Listening to these revelations, Sonja decided she wanted to talk to him in greater depth.

Maybe they could even tailor the searches according to the circumstances Ivan had seen in his shamanic state of consciousness. She also understood why he had this sense of ownership of the cave.

The first day of the exams

Concern was written on his face when Maxime walked into the exam hall with Ivan. As they approached, sweat filmed Ivan's palms and the back of his neck. An invigilator barked, "Name."

Ivan swallowed and stuttered. "Ivan Yezhov, sir."

"Front row right-hand side, right in front of the invigilator, so there can be no cheating."

Maxime took a deep breath and was about to object, but Ivan shook his head. "I'm fine. Thanks for the lift."

"Remember, stay in the hall until I pick you up."

Ivan walked slowly but deliberately to the front of the hall and his desk. Everyone seated followed his progress, but he looked ahead. Sitting down, Ivan glanced at the pad of paper with the university logo at the top. He carefully placed his pens and pencil along the top of the desk and sat back.

The invigilator walked around the students placing their question papers in front of them. "Don't open the questions, but check the title to know you have the correct document.

Ivan felt the panic rising. Could he do this? Why was he even here?" He was saved from a downward spiral by remembering he owed so much to Sonja and the cave spirits. He had to do the best he could. He breathed the same pattern he used when he went into his shamanic trance. Soon he felt calm at the command to open papers.

As he read the questions, he was transported to the

farmhouse and everything familiar. He remembered one of the students asking this very question. He remembered the answer. Picking up his pen, he wrote slowly, working through each question, hardly hearing the "Five minutes to go."

Walking slowly to the back of the hall, Ivan glanced out and fleetingly saw a small man dressed in black disappearing round the corner and down a corridor as Maxime walked along from the opposite direction. He was glad now about having to stay in the hall. He wondered if he had been waiting outside or walking along the corridor. He might have met with an accident.

"Prof, did you see that man dressed in black as you came along the corridor? When I reached the doors, I saw a short guy in black trousers and jacket hurry off around that corner." Ivan pointed to the other end of the hall, where the corridor was divided into two.

Maxime shook his head. "No, I saw nothing but that doesn't mean Yagor wasn't hanging around hoping to bump into you accidentally."

"That's what I thought too. I'm glad you told me to wait inside the hall."

"Hm, I'll deal with this. There's no need to tell Sonja. She is already worried."

Chapter 7

Mid-Winter

New Life

Every evening a dense mist swirled, taking visibility down to inches and with the snow thickly layered moving along the pathway was a treacherous exercise. Any unwary step and you could end up buried in a snowdrift. But these young men had grown up in this climate. They were used to these dangers. Under these conditions, they again agreed to journey from the present cave to that other many years ago. They were wrapped against the cold, but that did not stop their noses from turning red and hurting, They wore thick socks and fur-lined boots, and their jackets were also lined with sheepskin. Ivan thought they probably wore similar clothes to their ancient ancestors. The only difference would be that theirs were machine-stitched, and the ancients had to make all their garments by hand.

After endless discussions, Ivan's enthusiasm infected Vlad and his brother Piotr. Their talk about them could be mistaken for a conversation of contemporaries. They felt a similar sense of kinship as that Ivan had already experienced.

Vlad laughed, "Wouldn't it be strange if we find they are our ancestors?"

Piotr guffawed, "Not a chance. Look at how small you are, and that thigh bone was massive. I thought each generation got taller, but you must have shrunk." He tipped his head to the side and said. " Although Ivan might be, he's much taller than us."

"Come on, guys, this is a serious exploration. It works best if we approach it in the right frame of mind."

Vlad smiled and looked at his brother, miming a long face and a finger at his lips.

In the dim light, they scrambled into the places where they could use their instruments while leaning against the cave's back wall. To combat the cold and to create the right atmosphere, they wrapped blankets around their shoulders and had a fire burning in a little three-legged cast iron pot. Ivan spread a couple of blankets on the surface of a door. As he crouched down before stretching out, he thought the three occupied more space here than they could in his tiny room at the farmhouse.

A little self-consciously at first, they started playing the drum and the rattle as Ivan lay on a blanket staring up into the dark ceiling. By now, Ivan had moved into his shamanic state of consciousness quickly. He easily managed any obstacles and arrived at his cave entrance.

He looked about, puzzled. There was no sign of Aiee and her baskets. Unusual as the sun had not yet set. Previously, he had seen her work until it was almost dark, then packing her work implements and moving to the back of the cave to her hearth. Ivan looked about. He knew they did not leave the cave often because it was wintertime. He gasped as someone lifted the Auroch skin curtain. A lone hunter came in carrying a snow-white arctic hare. It was Een. He made his way to his hearth. Ivan followed and saw Aiee and Kitam together in the little shelter.

Thick snow cloaked the land outside. Few hunters would go out late in the afternoon in snow that deep. Ivan frowned as he observed the man skin and gut the little animal before wrapping it in dried leaves and burying it deep in the warm ash of the hearth. Ivan's attention swung back to the women. Aiee had been lying on the bracken bed, thrashing around. Now she was squatting and making guttural noises while she clung to Kitam. Ivan recalled some photos in a book and realised he was observing Aiee give birth. There were two other women present.

Kitam beckoned the woman, "Support Aiee while I get something to help with her pains."

They willingly linked arms around the writhing woman. Ivan wondered if it was right to be watching. Could it be construed as an intrusion? However, as he was invisible, he reasoned this would be valuable information. He saw Kitam delve into a curious bag and withdraw a pouch. He had seen these before. They were made from the intestines of one of their kills. Depending on how they were stitched, they make waterproof tubes or pouches. She shook some leaves into a gourd cup and added warm water from one of Aiee's woven baskets while changing the stone for another from the fire.

She turned back to the labouring woman, "Aiee, sip this. It will help the pains and allow the baby to come easily."

Since there was a pause between contractions, Kitam told the support ladies to lay their patient back on the bed. She reached out long slender fingers and gently palpated the woman's abdomen.

She nodded to an assistant, "Kneel and sit back on your heels with your knees apart." The one who had been on Aiee's left did as Kitam directed, while the other and Kitam helped Aiee to sit on the assistant's knees. Kitam nodded, "Good, now you support her back while I'll be here in front of Aiee."

Kitam knelt in front, making a strange tableau. As he watched, Ivan could see Aiee's face puckered up. Sweat poured off her forehead. She was pushing down hard. The back support companion wiped her head with a small piece of rabbit fur. Ivan wondered if there was any significance in using the fur. Then he remembered the babies of this cave wore rabbit skin, which he presumed was the equivalent of a modern nappy. They worked like this for some time, and Ivan felt anxious. He wondered if there was a problem. Then he heard Kitam command Aiee, "Push hard next time you feel the tightness."

Aiee nodded and gasped for breath. She took in a big breath. Her face screwed up again, then went red. As that happened, he saw Kitam lean down and pull gently while rotating the baby's head. There was a wet, slurping sound as a baby slithered into Kitam's waiting hands.

Tears were coursing down Ivan's face. He had witnessed animals give birth. He helped many of the sheep, but this was different. This was the birth of another human. He watched as Kitam gently laid the baby on a rabbit's skin while she felt it all over. Nodding her head, she placed the baby on her mother's tummy. At first, Aiee's face wreathed in smiles. Then it contorted again as Ivan watched, his eyes widened, and he felt a tension in his midriff. What could be wrong? However, it did not disturb Kitam, who expertly caught something as it slithered out of the woman. She placed it on the mother too. This was the afterbirth. Ivan was amazed as he watched the umbilical cord pulse firmly until, over time, it stopped. At that moment, Kitam using rawhide, quickly tied then cut the cord. By now, the baby was a lovely rosy colour. He thought back to the sheep birthing. They did not appear to have pain like this woman. However, it was all over quickly once the mother held her baby. Aiee lay back on the bed, cuddling her newborn daughter in her arms. Soon the tiny mite's head was bobbing around until it latched onto Aiee's nipple. She looked warm as she suckled from her mother.

Only now did Ivan look around the cave and the inhabitants' activities. They were busy with small tasks, not moving around. He wondered if this was how they conserved their energy in this bitterly cold weather. He was grateful, for although he considered the winters in this area severe, they did not come close to what these people endured.

Ivan was not conscious of time passing. Although he had not left the cave, he knew it was a few days later. Once again, he watched Kitam assist at another birth. The mother had her hair tied in a knot at the top of her head. Ivan understood that to mean the woman was a hunter. She was a fit, healthy young woman, and the labour seemed to progress well. As he observed, the birthing appeared to follow a similar pattern to the other one. Soon the huntress also delivered a healthy baby girl.

Kitam smiled at the mother and child, "Let the little one suckle now, and all will be well. I'll see you in the morning." Knowing her involvement was over, for now, she retired to her hearth.

On reflection, Ivan noticed that all the children seemed to be born about this time of the year. It made a lot of sense, as the mothers would not be out in the freezing weather. They would not be tramping around the countryside foraging since they made provision for this season and would have saved and preserved food to carry them through these lean times. He watched a man pull aside the Auroch curtain and leave the cave. He was not holding a spear or bow and arrow, therefore not intent on doing a little hunting. Ivan followed him and watched in astonishment as he squatted down on a small projection of the rock face, moved a lump of rock out of the way, thrust his arm into the space, and withdrew what looked like a large chunk of well-frozen meat. So these cave dwellers even had a deep freeze! He looked around to see if he could locate this store. It could mean another area for the team to search in the spring. He noted it was on the same level as the entrance to the cave and appeared to be a narrow ledge.

As Ivan watched, another man came and fished in the larder for more meat. The two men carefully wedged the stone firmly in the aperture. They intended to prevent any animals from being able to shift the rock and steal their winter stockpile. He looked to see if he could locate this useful larder. It must be a separate cave, but how did they keep things frozen? When they made a kill, it would be warm. How did they freeze it? Excited, he knew this was a mystery that needed exploring.

Back in the cave, Ivan stayed out of the way as he observed the men making a fire using a drill bow on dry tinder in the communal hearth. Soon little flickers of flame sprang into life. They fed it carefully until they had a fire burning merrily. First, they wrapped the meat in leaves. He watched as Enn called to a man sitting at a fireplace near the fire, "Bring the wrapping stuff." He quickly carried a bowl containing a thick white substance. The other cook and Een then covered the hunks of meat, which they spooned out with their hands from the wooden bowl. Ivan wondered if this might be clay. This was another thing to report to Sonja.

Een said, "Scrape the ashes to the side and dig there." He pointed as they buried it below the hot ashes. The women placed more foodstuffs on a rock to await the time to put it in the fire. Ivan thought, "This must be a celebratory meal, maybe for the safe birth of two more community members."

As he contemplated the need to report these happenings to Sonja, he travelled back instantly. Vlad, who had been watching him closely, stopped drumming immediately. Ivan lay on the blanket a little longer to get his bearings, then sat up and smiled at his friends. "That was fantastic. I went back to the people's cave and watched two births. I also saw where they stored their winter meat. They were getting a fire ready to cook it. Once this snow melts, I want to look for it."

"Well, while you have been whizzing around in ancient times, we've been getting cold, so I think it's time we went back to the farmhouse, and you made us a hot drink. That reminds me, do you know if they had hot drinks then?"

Piotr snorted. "Don't ask silly questions. How could they without saucepans?"

Ivan smiled. "You are right; they didn't have saucepans made of metal like us, but yes, they had hot drinks."

Vlad exclaimed, "Really! How could they heat water?"

Ivan continued, "They used tightly woven baskets which are waterproof. One birth I just witnessed was Aiee, the woman who weaves these baskets. They filled them with water and, at the same time, placed a few stones into it from the fire. When the stone was hot, the people carefully put them into the basket. By continuously changing the hot stones, it was possible to bring the water up to boiling. I guess that's how they could also make stewed food too."

The brothers looked at each other, and then Vlad said, "These guys were quite smart but not as smart as us."

Ivan shook his head. "We're not smart. We rely on lots of things around us, though. For instance, do you know how to make clothes? Could you make a weapon and catch your food? Do you know all about how your truck works?"

"No, but I can always look it up on Google."

"Exactly, Do you know how Google works or even your phone?"

"No, I take your point, they were smarter than us, but we collectively have better technology. Now, please, let's get that hot drink in the farmhouse. I'm freezing out here now the fire has died down."

A few days later, Sonja phoned. "Hello Ivan, how are you guys faring in this weather? At least the sheep can stay in the warmth, but that probably means a lot more work for you.

Thanks for the note you sent about observing the births. That's so interesting that they have their babies in winter. I wonder what they do to control that."

"Sonja, I also saw them getting food out of a deep freeze. I can't think how they convert recently killed meat into chunks of deeply frozen meat. It looks the same as when my mum gets out a roast."

The line crackled. She had to raise her voice. "Ivan, I think we are due a slight thaw soon. When that happens, I'll come out. We can talk about these findings further. I'm also hoping your exam results will be out by then too."

Chapter 8

Results

There was a constant drip from the eaves as the snow retreated. Sonja's vehicle rattled into the yard, Ivan was in the barn as it was too cold to take the sheep out, but he was engrossed with his chores. She stuck her head through the doors calling, "Ivan, Ivan, come quickly. Here's the envelope with your results. Let's see how well you've done."

Reluctantly Ivan left the warmth of the old building. He was not sure if he wanted to open the envelope. What if he'd failed? What if he'd let Sonja down? What about the spirits in the cave? As if it contained poison, Ivan took the envelope, and they walked into the kitchen. She noted his hands trembled, and he had a rapid blink.

To console him, she put her arm over his shoulder and could feel his trembling. "Come on, lad. I'm sure you've done well. I know how important this is to you. Why don't you read the letter in your room while I grab a cup of tea? You must come and tell me as soon as you're in control. I'm sure it will be good, but if not, tell me anyway, and we can talk."

With clammy hands, he held the letter and walked to his room or doom like a man condemned approaching the scaffold.

Sitting at the old table and talking nonsense to the farmer's wife, Sonja thought that time had slowed. She was tense without noticing her shoulders were near her ears. She was sitting there listening out for his return.

Her heart sank when she heard the slow footsteps coming down the corridor. Had it all come to nothing? All the hopes she had for him? The new life she wanted for him, all gone? She had the urge to cry but thought that would be unfair to Ivan. The door creaked as it opened slowly. He moved into the room, Head down, his face impassive, the image of total defeat and thrust the letter at her. She scanned it, then yelled, "Oh Ivan, you've cracked it! Well done. This calls for a celebration." She flung her arms around him. The farmer's wife joined in with the group hug. She peeled off, saying, "I'll bake a celebratory cake," as she grabbed her apron off the back of the kitchen chair.

Vlad and Piotr came over as if by osmosis, happy to add their congratulations. Soon the cake was sitting on the rack cooling.

Sonja said, "I think you better come back to town with me after we have called in to your parents to let them know the good news. Can anyone look after the sheep?"

Piotr said, "I'm free now and happy to take over for a few days while you visit the city lights." He was secretly pleased as once Ivan did move. There would be a regular job here for him.

Sonja drove Ivan to his parent's place. "I'll wait in the van for you."

He ran down the path to their house. Breathless, he banged on the door, "Mum, Dad are you here?" Of course, they were. "I've passed my exams! I can go to university to study archaeology!"

His mother wiped a tear away with her apron. "I always

knew you could do it, my boy."

His grin split his face as he said, "I'm going back to town now with Sonja. She said she could employ me, so although I won't send you a shepherd's wage, I will still send money for the girls."

The girls crowded into the little sitting room, each trying to pat and congratulate him. Amidst the babble of voices, he said, "I have to go now as Sonja is waiting, but I'll see you all soon."

On the journey to the city, Ivan said, "Sonja, do you think I was wrong observing those women giving birth?"

She thought for a moment, then said, "Ivan, think about the situation. Nowadays, if you were studying with a gynaecologist, you would be expected to attend births. The women would accept your presence as a professional. Your observing is the same kind of thing. You are working on their behalf. Now tell me all about what you observed. Think carefully. You must also have observed all the actions, not just the birth. Please give me a sense of the surroundings. How did they see what they were doing? What time of the day was it? You knew it was winter. Why? What did you see? What was the temperature, not in numbers like on a thermometer, but what clothing did they wear? What were they using for heating?"

His eyebrows shot up, and he barked a spontaneous laugh. "Wow, you don't expect much, do you?"

She said, "If you went into a maternity ward today to observe a birth, you would come back, and I would expect a full report. So far, you have fixed on the main protagonists in the drama, that's good, but you will have absorbed the stuff happening around you too. You are in a unique position to be able to make real a world we know very little about. We can only build up a picture from tiny fragments of fossils, yet you have seen it in glorious technicolour and detail. Of course, I want you to report every aspect. Things like did they store food and clothing? If so, where? In what? You have told me about the heating baskets. Did they also use baskets for storage? They put meat on the fire. How did they share it? Was there a free for all fight or sharing? Who fed first? Women and children or the men."

He sat thoughtfully for a while before answering. "I will have to train myself to take in the bigger picture, not just home in on one action. I can't answer most of those questions."

She smiled to herself. Then she said, "These shamanic journeys are not entertainment. You have a powerful gift which can inform and direct so much. That is how your spirits can become real people to us today."

He sighed. "Sounds like a lot of work for me."

She nodded. "Yes, that's why you are going to train to be an archaeologist, don't worry, you will create lots of work for us too, enough of being serious. You will stay with my parents for a few days as you did before. I've already told them we are coming, and guess what?"

He laughed and said, "Your mother is organising a dinner party. Can I guess who the guests will be?"

She looked over at him. "Yes, Mother likes Mikhail and Zoya. You will have to retell this last journey to them as well."

Over the celebratory dinner, they listened to his report then a hubbub of questions tumbled out.

Zoya said, "You say they stored food outside the cave, but it looked frozen. How?"

He shrugged. "I don't know. I wondered if it could be another small cave. I did look at the surroundings, though."

Sonja was excited as that might answer how these hunter-gatherers survived the long, cold winter months in such severe conditions. This alone showed these people were not a collection of stupid, ignorant people just clinging onto life but highly intelligent, well-organised people able to make plans and survive in difficult circumstances like the long, bitterly cold winters.

Mikhail grinned. "We'll all have to explore with you in the spring to find this storage place."

Maxime sat back and smiled. This young man was so full of promise. His "visions" were capable of redirecting all their talents. He hadn't seen Sonja and her friends so excited since their student days.

Sonja asked, "You said you think they gave birth in the winter. What made you think that?"

Ivan thought a moment and closed his eyes as if to relive the experience. "Well, I saw two births in quick succession, and the other children seemed to vary in age but in groups, like in a school. That made me think like the sheep. There must be a birthing time."

Mikhail said, "I wonder if the light intensity affects fertility? We live with so much artificial lighting now. Has that made us different? I need to speak to Korgai and find out when his people tend to give birth."

Zoya wondered, "Ivan, if you found this storage place could I explore it? There might be fossils, which could prove useful in my research."

The following morning as they sat drinking coffee in the kitchen, Sonja said, "Ivan, last night was so exciting talking about all the possibilities. I think you must be careful with who you share these insights. Don't feel you have to let anyone into this. You are only starting on your academic route, but many people would exploit your discoveries and insights, and I suspect not to your or "your people's" benefit. Of course, that does not include Zoya and Mikhail. Think carefully and check out the credentials of anyone wanting information or to join you exploring."

Once he returned to the farm, Ivan planned a longer visit to his family. He missed having Bone following him around. As he walked along the path from the bus stop, he looked out onto the field, and there was his friend Bone standing, poking his head through the wire.

"Hello, Bone, good to see you. I presume this is your harem. How many do you have in your flock now?" He could see half a dozen sheep grazing. He smiled. There were so many changes here at home and in his life, all thanks to this crazy sheep.

His exam results delighted his mother. "I'm sorry you had to go so quickly after giving us your results. I always knew you could do well. I felt so guilty when you had to leave school. Now I know you'll be a great success in your studies. One day I would like to meet this lady who's done so much for you. What's her name again?"

He was unsure he wanted to show Sonja how poor his home was, although his mother kept it clean. Since Bone came to them, there had been an improvement in their finances. People paid for Bone to cover their ewes so they could boast about the connection to the famous ram. Also, now she had sheep's milk every day, and his mother could make cheese for sale too.

As Ivan sat on the bus going back to the farm, he thought about how his life had changed, all because a lamb got lost and a human bone was found. Now he could study and get a qualification. He smiled. It was all thanks to Sonja taking an interest in him and giving him those books.

Chapter 9

Preparing for a Hunt

"Ivan, how about we visit your folks? Our cookie tin is empty, and your Mum's cookies are the best." Vlad suggested.

Ivan nodded, "Yes, that's fine, but I think this is a typical case of cupboard love."

Ivan and Vlad left school together at the end of their primary school years. They had different reasons for leaving. Ivan had three younger sisters, and money was tight, but Vlad and Piotr were orphans. They lived on the next-door farm, and Vlad worked for his distant relative farmer for many years. The farmer felt giving the boys a tiny room and old clothes left over by his children showed generosity. Vlad willingly paid what little he earned for their board and lodging, so Piotr stayed at school a bit longer.

Vlad and Ivan's dad wandered off to look at the sheep. The flock was slowly growing. Vlad commented, "It's hard to believe that one little lamb could make such a difference to so many of us. I love the drumming and helping Ivan with his shamanic studies; of course, we get to glimpse the ancient people of the cave. Now I also feel quite possessive about them. I wouldn't like to do all that trance stuff like Ivan. It's spooky. "

As usual, at the end of their visit, Ivan's Mum sent them off with a couple of boxes of biscuits.

"Here, you take one tin back with you, and we'll hide the other in my room. The farmer's wife gives the other cave workers enough anyway."

Once again, the guys went down to the cave. "Ivan, I'll get the rest of our kit ready if you light the fire."

Ivan wiggled the board around to ensure he would be comfortable before covering it with an old blanket.

Sonja suggested they keep the board and trance stuff in the cave to save them from carrying it back and forth. Ivan listened to Vlad as he beat the drum fast, even and relentlessly, allowing him to drift away into yet another journey, drawing Ivan further and further down into the earth, the tunnels, and the spirit world.

Ivan felt the thrill of being back in his cave, but now there appeared to be visitors. They were milling around the open entrance area. These were ferocious-looking, stocky people, most with dark hair drawn back and tied with rawhide into long ponytails or caught up into tight knots held with long wooden pins. Their dark eyes were noticeably different from the cave folk with their brown hair, which tended to be curly or downright frizzy, and pale blue eyes.

Unseen, Ivan moved easily among them, trying to understand what was happening. Since the talk with Sonja, he made an effort to notice all the elements of the bigger picture, not just the exciting actions. There was an air of expectancy and tension. Their hands unconsciously stroked the blades of their spears and tested the sharpness of their arrowheads. With a jolt, Ivan noticed they were all hunters, there were no children, and the women present were not mothers but also hunters.

He wondered if these could be the people who owned

the arrowhead the excavation crew had found near the cave mouth all those months ago. Maybe they were some of the inhabitants of that other cave? The one where he and Vlad had located the other three arrowheads. He felt that was possible when he noticed the resemblance between these people and the weaver Aiee. He surmised that she had come to this cave to marry Een. The cooperation between the two groups was evident. The hosts were interspersed among the visitors. Soon Een suggested they all sit to talk. Ivan wondered if they were planning to go to war or if it was a hunt. If so, they must cooperate to bring down some large prey, maybe a woolly rhinoceros or even a mammoth. They all sat around the central hearth, enjoying an evening meal and murmuring. This must be something serious, as there was no laughter. Silence fell as they rolled up in their pelts and settled to sleep.

The next day, as Ivan watched, even more hunters arrived and squeezed into the cave. They sat around the central hearth and discussed the upcoming hunt while checking their weapons. The knappers were hard at work, chipping here and there to ensure the sharpest blades and points.

Ivan was so in tune with these people that, like their shaman, there was very little need for language. He understood they were planning an ambitious hunt, which usually only happened once in a generation because of the dangers. They wanted to pit their stone-tipped weapons against the biggest animal in their world, the woolly mammoth.

One of the visitors said, "I remember the story told by the shaman of the hunt my grandfather went on, which was also near here. A gully leads to good grazing and abundant water, or the mammoths could choose to go a long way around by going onto the plain to the right of the ravine."

A local hunter nodded his head. "Yes, we know the one

you are meaning. It's not far from our cave."

Another said, "Enough of the remembering. Let's get on with the planning."

The rest of the cave inhabitants were up and about, busy with their morning chores. The children were going mad with the excitement of visitors. In their opinion, it was just extra special because there were no visiting children to dilute the adult's attention.

The hunters focused their attention once again on the job at hand.

"How can we make them go down the ravine instead of fanning out onto the plain."

A smart one had a bright idea. "Easy, we split the herd and make a section stamped down between the cliffs."

Another humphed. "How do we do that? Stand and wave our arms around?"

An intelligent answer came from one of the visitors. "That's not a bad idea, but we need to look like the scenery, like a tree or a rock or something."

"That might work, but we would need to be upwind of them, so how do we manage that too?"

Another ignored that last statement and said, "We could carry rocks, big ones and hide behind them."

A visitor snorted at his companion. "How do you plan to move a stone which will make the mammoths change course?"

The other shrugged, "I don't know. It just seemed a good idea."

An excited hunter interrupted the beginning of an argument. " That's not a bad idea, but instead of rock, why don't we dress, so we look like trees?"

That concept took root, and in the end, they decided to bind branches together and weave thin twigs to make a moveable panel shielding them from sight.

"So we hide behind the

The level of excitement rose until, eventually, they were all talking at once about how to go about this idea.

Een put up his hands. "Enough, only one person talks at a time; otherwise, no one knows what is going on. So far, we have agreed we will make barriers from saplings and woven leaves. All very well, but who will be behind these? And how do we plan to make the mammoths stampede?"

One slightly more mature guy said, "I think if we make a noise, that should spook them. They're not fond of cave lions. Can anyone make a sound like their roar?"

Slowly the ideas took shape, and then the leader of the visiting hunters said. "I think we can sum it up like this, we make barriers, and some of us go well behind the herd and make a noise, maybe like a lion if not just a racket. Hopefully, that will start a stampede among at least a segment, if not the whole herd. Then what do we want?"

The older hunter again said, "Once they are running between the cliffs, it should be easy to separate a calf to the edge of the group and drive it down that blind alley."

One of Een's hunters pulled a face and said, "Then what? We stand like a reception committee and stick out our spears.? Why don't we use the usual method of digging a big hole, covering it and driving one of the beasts into it?"

One of the hunters heaved a great sigh, "Where's the challenge in that? Surely we can come up with a new way to hunt? If we can get a calf, there should be enough meat for both caves to carry us through the winter. The hunter we think the best gets to win the hide."

They all nodded, picturing how they would look with such a prized pelt.

While the hunters were having this serious debate, two little girls were hunting each other through the cave, screaming and shouting, more than excited. So many people were in one place. One child, Ina, was dark-eyed and raven-haired. She was the child of Aiee. The other, Chen, was born two days after Ina to the hunter couple amid these discussions. The visitors marvelled at her pale skin and ice-blue eyes. Eventually, her mother called, "Chen ....

Two of the host hunters were a couple with a three-year-old girl, Chen. She, together with her friend Ina, ran around, screaming excitedly. She did not understand the danger but was enjoying all the extra attention from these new hunters who bounced her on their laps and marvelled at her pale skin and ice-blue eyes. At last, her Mother called, "Chen, come. You must sleep now. We all have to leave very early in the morning."

Ivan watched as the full moon hung high in the sky, its silvery light reaching far into the crowded cave. Guta and his father looked at each other, "It's time we spoke to the spirits."

They made their way to the back of the cave. As they passed Gutas's hearth, Kitam called him across and handed him a hollowed-out gourd with some dark liquid swishing around at the bottom. She whispered, "I thought you would want to talk to the spirits, so I made this for you. It is the drink my Mother and I used to make for the shaman at home. Carry it carefully and only have it when you are at your seeing place."

He looked questioningly at her, "You never told me about this before. What is it?"

"I didn't think it necessary to say anything, but when

I saw the herbs while we were out collecting this time, I brought some back. There are very few of them around. Our shaman said it helped them move into the other worlds more easily."

He nodded, "We'll try it, thank you. My special wife, I'm so happy you're mine. I must go now, but please look after my Mother."

She nodded and gently pushed him away, "Be careful and don't spill any. Now go."

As usual, they squeezed their way through the narrow fissure at the back of the main cave and along the twisting passage, finally having to feel for the low entrance. Then they bent low and wriggled through, emerging into the sacred cave. As usual, they did this in the dark but carried a torch and tinder for light this time. Guta also carefully took the hollowed gourd. Ivan accompanied them, experiencing none of their discomforts. When younger, Guta had feared this journey, but now he understood it was all part of the ritual. Once in their sacred cave, Guta lit the torch while his father sniffed suspiciously at the dark liquid. Guta explained it was the stuff that the shaman from Kitam's clan used.

The older man nodded, remembering how that shaman had quickly gone into the trance state and seemed to see much more vividly than all the others, but for all that, he had still not achieved the status of Guta's father. Dialogue between the two of them They decided one would take it and one would do it the old way. Guta knew he would be the one doing the drinking. He thought how cunning his father was to put off trying anything new. Nevertheless, Guta swallowed the stuff. At first, it made him gag, and then nausea hit. He wanted to retch but knew this was a typical reaction to the drink. Slowly as nausea receded, he looked around and blinked. The cave looked different. The painted images on the wall were undulating as if they had come to life. As if, at last, they had travelled through the stony veil and were with them in the cave. Now he knew he was ready to go to the spirit world.

Ivan watched as they sat, swaying backwards and forwards, chanting and clapping out a rhythm that slowly became faster. Ivan was very grateful for the help Vlad's drumming gave him to reach the spirits. This way seemed so much harder and, from the looks on their faces, quite a painful exercise.

Over time, their breathing became shallower and quicker, and then they felt their power rise in their spines and explode in their heads. Guta felt the familiar sensation of being stretched, wrapping his whole body with pain and pins and needles. He climbed the liana rope, which he saw dangling in front of him. When he reached the top, he saw the big-eyed spirits approach. From this new perspective, he looked around for his father and saw him far away, like a tiny figure climbing up a steep ladder. He wanted to stretch out and pull him up but knew he could not reach him that way. Instead, he sent his intention out, and it was as if his father had gained wings. He rose swiftly and stood beside his son, looking around.

What he now saw dazed the old man. It was as if previously he had seen through a mist, which was now clear. They asked the spirits about the possibility of a child for Guta and received what they thought was a positive but confusing response. The spirits showed them a vision. From that, the shaman understood Guts's child was already born to another woman, but the child would be with him soon and that Kitam was the real Mother. There were other things to ask, too, like how was the baby they had buried. The spirits never gave direct answers, but Guta and his father understood the gift the little one had brought was acceptable, and that was why Guta would have another child soon.

Then they asked the spirits for a blessing on the hunt in the morning. Unexpectedly both men experienced pain. They writhed on the floor of the cave. Suddenly there was blood everywhere. They were confused as the spirits were no longer visible either. Ivan observed their pain, yet not being part of the ritual, did not feel this phenomenon. However, like them, he saw the blood. He blanched. It was as if there was a lake of thick sticky stuff.

Neither they nor Ivan could understand these strange signs but interpreted them as an omen. The hunt would be successful. The pain and the absence of the spirits at the end were confusing. This had never happened before. The two could not come up with an explanation other than as a blessing on the hunt.

Both men were so confused that they decided it was time to return. Hours later, the older man shook Guta, lying on the cave floor, to say they must return to the cave soon. Guta took longer than usual to wake up and be able to think. They talked about this strange news of a child but decided to say nothing of their journey to anyone, especially Kitam. They would continue their everyday activities. Kitam was still waiting for them, "Did you speak to the spirits? I feel strange, and oddly enough, I am uncomfortable. Maybe it is because we have so many hunters. I don't know all of them."

Chapter 10

The Hunt

The two young men sat in Ivan's room, talking. "Vlad, I'm sure they're preparing for a hunt. I feel as if I'm there with them all the time. Could you and Piotr come over every evening after work until we know what's going on?"

Vlad was every bit as excited as Ivan about the events going on in the cave.

"Of course." Tilting his head on one side and drawing his lips together, he said, "We'll come by truck. It'll save a bit of time."

Ivan's shoulders dropped. Then Vlad realised how tense he was about the unfolding drama in the cave.

Sonja was so fascinated by the story he related that she phoned every morning to get an update on the activities they had observed. She asked about Ivan's insights, like the arrowheads and the different appearances of the visitors. She planned to do an in-depth search of the other cave for bone fragments. If they could identify a difference through the DNA, then again, Ivan's unorthodox methods were justified.

The lads settled in their usual places at the back of the cave. The drumming and the rattle guided Ivan into the shamanic state of consciousness. He saw the typical barrow-like mound of earth with its hole at the top. Unerringly, he went down like a fish diving deep into the water. He flew through the tunnel, emerging into "his" cave.

Once there, the tension was palpable. Ivan knew the scouts had seen the mammoths heading towards the area where the hunters wanted them. It was early in the season, and all of them were hardly out of the winter torpor, but suddenly everyone in the cave was excited and busy. As Ivan had observed the day before, the hunters were still checking their weapons, and the nappers rapped out a staccato beat as they chipped more points for spears and arrows. The hunters from the other cave joined them in this almost frenzied activity.

The night before, the hunters and helpers made a plan to divert the herd. The helpers planned to slip out and cut saplings to create the barriers they intended to use to block the massive animals' progress and encourage them to go into the valley. Ivan watched as they slipped out of the cave and down the narrow path. He followed them as they moved stealthily along. He felt this would be an important exercise for two reasons. One to see how they prepared for such a momentous undertaking and two so he could identify the area that would allow modern humans to search for any detritus from this undertaking.

Once back in the cave, as he watched, he subconsciously understood the meaning of their gestures and language, not with his hearing faculties. The leader said, "We must pile this stuff at the entrance. It will be easier to carry all the bits and make them up when we are there. We'll still have time before the herd gets anywhere near."

Another nodded in agreement. "But I think we should each take what we need rather than one carrying all the poles and another the creeper for tieing."

"Yes, that's good. I hope you all cut enough for the stuff to go round. We could still gather more when we are there if we need it. Remember, you must make the screen big enough to cover you but not so high the hunters behind can't see the prey."

Gita walked among them and helped allocate the bits into piles, ready for the morning.

One of the hunters asked, "Guta, have the spirits blessed this enterprise?"

Guta said, "Don't worry, my father and I will visit the spirits later this evening to ask for their blessing."

Ivan heard the sharp drum beats calling him back. Disappointed, he returned to the modern-day cave and his friends.

He blinked his eyes. "Hi, guys. Thanks, that was awesome. I followed the hunter helpers to where they went to cut saplings, ready to make the barriers. The cave is crazy, everyone preparing their weapons like spears and arrows."

Piotr yawned. "What barriers are you talking about?"

"They plan on tying saplings and leaves to create a barrier to hide behind. Once there, they'll make a noise and hope the mammoths will veer into the valley. They hope a calf will get lost and go down the blind ally."

"Gee, that's lots of hopes, but I suppose they don't have guns and things like we have now."

The next evening when Ivan went on his trance journey, he returned to the cave. He saw it was early in the morning on the day of the hunt. The sky had still not lightened. He observed the tension in the hunters as they kept checking their weapons. While others were checking their arrows, they stroked the edges of their spears to ensure the sharpness had not disappeared overnight. Did they have sufficient? Was the bowstring tight enough? That's when he saw the precious arrowhead fall, the one they would find so many thousands of years later. The owner had not noticed its loss. However, Ivan recognized the hunter as one from the other cave. That minor incident would have enormous repercussions. Now Ivan felt he could prove their hypothesis about the people of the other cave. He knew it would need scientific validation, but they were on the right track.

In absolute silence, carrying all they needed, they filed out of the cave. Their steps made no sound as they carefully picked their way along the pathway into the little valley below, and then they all made off toward the designated hunting area. The rest of the cave inhabitants would only come after the hunt concluded. They would wait until they received the signal. They did the butchering, then carting it back to the storage place near the cave and preparing and cooking the meat for a feast.

As Ivan observed, some scouts confirmed the herd was on the move. Now the assistants had to make a noise to stop the animals from spreading out. First, they had to funnel them towards the valley. Then they had to force them to stampede down it. Only in that kind of situation would the hunters be able to separate a calf and drive it into the ravine and towards the points of the waiting spearmen. So long as the herd was calm and walked, the calf would stay close to its mother, and she could defend it. The people could not afford for that to happen.

The barrier people carried the materials in the half-light of the dawning day, picking their way down the steep path. The air was chill, and they shivered in the light breeze but knew soon they would be sweating. Once on-site, they dumped the material in piles. The leader directed them. "Put the thick sapling branches here. There should be enough to make eight barriers. Four on each side."

Another helper said, "Where should we put the rawhide?"

The leader said, "I think we need to divide it into two piles, one for binding the framework and the other to use as the basis for weaving the thin twigs into a decent screen.

One of the workers suggested. "It would be easier if we worked in a circle then and had constructors and runner helpers to bring stuff they needed as they worked."

Their leader nodded in agreement. They were ready to work as the sun peeked over distant hills.

The scouts who planned to startle the lumbering giants were already making their way via a wide detour to get behind their quarry without them becoming anxious.

The killer hunters were moving into place at the blind end of the off-shoot ravine. Een was amongst these. He said, "We must take cover as best we can amongst these rocks. We can then spring out together as the animal comes down. We need as many spear points into the animal as possible. If we are lucky, someone can get a spear into its eye or under its throat."

Back out at the entrance, the barrier maker's screens were looking good. Their leader said, "Right, I want four of you on each screen, one on each side to hold the structure and two with spears at the ready. The spear holders must watch the movements of the animals. You move the screen to keep you all hidden from their sight if necessary.

Just beyond them, the bow and arrow hunters planned to stand on either side of the ravine and let their arrows go. They were aiming for the eyes too, and if they were lucky, the animal lifted its head to bellow the throat.

They were all keyed up, their eyes dilated, and their hearts thumped. Then they heard the yelling behind them and the thud of heavy feet starting to run.

The barrier group joined in with the noise as the herd came into view. The startled beasts tossed their heads back, their ears flattened, and their trunks reached forward. They started a rumbling trot. The barriers appeared to funnel them in the right direction. All the hunters smiled at each other. They could taste success. While the beaters leapt up and down and yelled, the animals panicked. Now more ran. It was like a river. At first, the herd moved slowly, then picked up speed. Once upset, the leading animals started trumpeting, echoing off the gorge's stone walls. The din and dust maddened them even more. All was going as planned.

Not one but two calves lost contact with their mothers and charged down the blind ravine. It encouraged the hunters. This was even better than they had hoped, but could they bring down the two? The rest of the herd went thundering along the gorge. The dust was so thick it was difficult to see. Once the barrier beaters had directed the calves towards the waiting spearmen, they relaxed. No one saw the angry matriarch, who noticed her calf was missing. She veered across the herd and charged down the ravine. The beaters only saw her as she loomed out of the dust, but that was too late. There was nowhere for them to escape. The din was so loud they could not warn the waiting spearmen or the bow and arrow hunters either. The matriarch was maddened by the noise, and her calf was missing. She did not slow down for the puny humans in front of her. The enraged animal, swinging her great head from side to side, caught one of the bowhunters, their best woman marksman. She had tried to shoot the beast in the eye to slow this behemoth but missed. The arrow merely irritated an already angry cow. Lowering her head, she caught the woman on the tip of her huge tusk and carelessly tossed her aside before continuing towards her calf.

The woman flew high in the air, the last sound she made,

her scream heard above the stampeding herd, and then her body fell in a heap, like a disjointed doll. The spearmen saw what was happening and tried scrabbling up the steep stony sides of the ravine. It was a vain attempt to escape since there was nowhere to go. The cow, swinging her trunk, tossed two of them aside while she speared another with her tusk. The milling calves trampled the hunters who might have escaped the angry adult.

The brave hunters lay still on the ground. Their spears snapped like twigs lying beside them. The mammoth matriarch had a prodigious memory. She remembered the exact layout of the ravine and drove the calves ahead as she returned to the herd that, by now, had quietened down but still kept running away.

An eerie silence followed. The few hunters who had survived the disaster ran towards their comrades. Two of the bow and arrow hunters lay dead, one from each group. Five spearmen also lay dead or close to dying, so severely injured that they had little chance of surviving.

The sudden change in the fortunes of these intrepid hunters appalled Ivan. He wished he could help, but he was still an unseen presence among them.

Kitam had stayed back at the cave with Aiee, but now one of the younger clan members ran up the path. He yelled. "Kitam, come quickly. It has all gone wrong. There are injured and dead hunters. Guta said, please hurry."

Without wasting a moment, she turned to Aiee. "Put as many bowls of water to heat as you can." She turned to the youngster. "Show me the quickest way." She dashed behind him as he leapt over rocks and gullies to take her by the shortest route, not caring about being silent now.

Kitam reached the shocked and silent group. Guta and his father were already there, having accompanied the hunters, but had not taken part in the action. Men carefully brought the dead to the opening of the ravine. The mammoths were long gone, so there was no danger. Kitam hurried up to her husband. "What happened? Are there any left alive?"

He nodded and indicated three with shocking injuries and two were not so bad. Kitam checked each one. She then opened her medicine bag and shook out some dried leaves and the powder from seeds, which she had ground very fine. She added these to a bit of water in a gourd cup. Hurrying over to the ones not likely to survive, she carefully dropped some drops into their mouths and stroked their throats to encourage them to swallow. A few moments later, their eyes closed. They breathed more easily now their pain had diminished.

Then she turned her attention to the other two, the possible survivors. She also gave a few drops and waited until they closed their eyes. She felt all over them to assess the extent of their injuries. Both had broken legs, but fortunately, the bone had not come through the skin. She needed to hold these limbs tight and transport the injured back to the cave. She looked around and saw a stand of birch trees not far off. Hurrying there, she called, "Quick, bring me a knife."

Twice she pulled chunks of bark off and cut them so she had two solid pieces in the tree's shape. These she carried back to her patients. Looking at the young messenger, she said, "Don't just stand there. Get me some water while I cut some of that creeper I saw as we were coming here."

The lad was panting as he carried the water, arriving at the same time as Kitam. "Here, help me wet the bark. Now hold the leg firmly."

He watched as she slipped it around the leg and tied it on with a length of the creeper. Once this satisfied her, she gave each patient more sleeping drops. Ivan trailed after her, marvelling at how efficiently she had felt the limbs and diagnosed the fractures. He hurried after her as she went back to the other three patients. One had died peacefully, one looked dazed, and the last one had peculiar breathing. She made sure someone was there to hold their hands as she told Guta that one had already died.

Ivan felt he was hovering over them, seeing the tragedy but unable to help or even commiserate with these devastated people. He watched as they carefully carried the newly dead hunter to where the others already lay. The shamans had been busy. Already they had rubbed red ochre on the faces and chests of the dead. Now they were ready for their last journey to the deathrock and then into the starry sky.

Everyone was silently standing around, too shocked to do anything. Kitam wasted no time. Quickly she organised some of them to carry two of the makeshift barriers over to the two warriors with the broken legs. Then she returned to her terminal patients. The one who was breathing oddly had silently slipped away into the arms of death. But the other one looked less dazed. He was one of the visiting hunters. She was sure he had internal injuries but decided to take the risk of moving him so she could look after him in the cave too. She had to ask for another barrier to use as a stretcher.

These actions impressed Ivan. He wanted to find out how modern medics managed. As their silent observer, Ivan watched as Kitam led her helpers carrying the three patients. Aiee, her daughter Inna, and little Chen were standing at the mouth of the cave. Kitam looked at Aiee, then at Chen and shook her head slightly. They laid the injured by the central hearth as there was more room for Kitam and her helpers to care for the patients.

Meanwhile, Chen kept asking when her parents would

return. As Guta came up the path, the little child yelled at him. He looked down at this anxious child through red-rimmed eyes, and it struck him. She had no parents anymore. He stopped, looked at her momentarily, and then put out his hand. "Come with me. We need to talk."

They walked away from the cave while he broke the news to her. Then they went to the death rock. The dead hunters lay arranged peacefully. She ran first to her mother. She touched the broken, unresponsive body. Then to her father, his eyes closed forever as he lay next to his wife. She knelt, touching them both and sobbed until Guta came and gently lifted her. "Come, child, they have a long way to go to the spirit world. We must not stop them."

"But I want my Amma. When will she come back to me?" The tears streamed down her cheeks. She did not understand.

While watching this painful exchange, Ivan felt tears coursing down his cheeks. He also felt as if his heart would break. He did not know until now that the emotions of those he observed impacted him so strongly.

He watched as Guta gently led Chen away down the path to the river. They sat on a big rock, watching the water tumbling past them until she stopped crying. Then he told her the story of how brave her parents had been. Now they had gone to continue the hunt in the spirit world.

Chen forgot to cry. "What does the spirit world look like?"

Guta spoke gently to the child, with love in his eyes, at great length about many things, especially about journeys to the spirit world. He explained the need for a shaman to act as the go-between for the people and the spirits.

Ivan listened to this conversation. It amazed him when in a serious tone, all trace of tears gone, she asked, "Can I speak to the spirits? Can I talk to my parents?"

Just as gravelly, he answered her. "Not everyone can talk to the spirits, which is why we have a shaman."

"But you are a shaman, so do you talk to them?"

"Yes, but it is difficult to reach the spirits. Often, they are difficult to understand."

"Why? Don't they talk like we are now? I've seen you go through the hole at the back of the cave. Is that where they live? Is that where Amma and Abba have gone?"

They seemed such sensible questions to Ivan. It was hard to believe they were from a three-year-old, but the tears came again. Ivan wanted to reach out to this newly orphaned child and Guta, trying to comfort her.

"Who will cook my food now?" Chen said. "I know about weaving from Inna's Amma, but I'm too small to hunt, and I don't know how to cook, so no one will want to marry me."

As Ivan continued to eavesdrop on this amazing conversation, he was surprised to hear Guta say, "You are only a child, so there is no need for you to marry for us to help. Kitam and I have no children. Would you like to come and live at our hearth? Then Kitam can cook for all of us, and when you are bigger, you could hunt with me."

Chen thought about this for a few moments, then nodded slowly. "But I might cry at night, and Kitam never laughs. She would be cross with me."

Guta smiled. "Kitam has a lot of things to think about and no child to make her happy. She would love to have you as our family."

As Ivan followed them along the path and watched them enter the cave, the little girl saw Kitam and ran over to her, "K'am, can I be your child?"

Everyone heard her. They all stopped to listen to the reply. Ivan held his breath along with the other inhabitants.

Slowly Guta acknowledged what the spirit world had meant when they said his child had already been born. He was to take on the responsibility of bringing up this orphaned girl.

Kitam smiled and held her arms towards the child, "Chen, I would love to have you as my child. Come, let me hug you."

From then on, the child was never far from Kitam. Soon the cave was calling her K'am since Chen could not pronounce her name, and it seemed fitting that as the new mother, she should have a new name too. Ivan smiled at this endearing quirk as the drumming called him back.

Vlad was perspiring. "What happened there, Ivan? I tried calling you back, but you rolled your head as if to say no, and you were crying at one point."

"That was the most moving experience I have ever had. I can't tell you about it just now, but I promise I will as soon as I have things sorted in my head. Come, let's go back to the farmhouse."

The next day when Ivan phoned Sonja, all he could say was, "Sonja, the journey last night was remarkable. The hunt was a massacre of the people. It has made me so emotional you deserve to hear this face-to-face. Also, there are loads of leads for the excavations. We need to explore places in the area."

Chapter 11

Meeting a Shaman

Ivan, as usual, was busy in the barn when he heard Sonja call him. He had not expected to see her quite so soon after his call. He thought he would have a little time to process the events he had witnessed. The terrible carnage had disturbed him greatly. He wondered if they could have done things differently and was concerned about the fate of the injured ones. Would Kitam be able to help them? He had to snap back to the present. It came as a surprise to see her peering around the door.

"Ivan, will you be much longer?"

He hurried over to her, "How come you're here? The roads are so awful?"

"Come on, Ivan, a little snow might stop others, but there's so much I want to share with you. Can you come yet?"

"I'll finish putting the feed in the pens. Then I can safely leave them."

As Ivan rounded the side of the barn, he saw another vehicle in the yard. Now all the visitors were inside. He hurried across and opened the door to the warm fug of the kitchen.

The farmer's wife was in her element, making tea and trying to feed everyone some of her baking.

Mikhail was talking to a tall man who stood with his back to the door, but as Ivan entered, the visitor swung around and fixed Ivan with a pair of icy blue eyes set in a brown, creased and weathered face. His skin looked like leather. He had tied his stringy grey hair with a rawhide thong into a ragged ponytail snaking down his back.

Mikhail called across the room, "Ah, Ivan, I've someone here who would like to meet you." Pointing to their guest, he continued, "This is Korgai. He's a Yugur shaman. When I told him about you and the cave, he asked if he could visit, maybe even do a ritual with you."

Ivan blushed. Here was an authentic shaman from Yurgur right up in the northern part of the country, and he wanted to work with him.

Vlad and Piotr had walked to their employer's farm as soon as it was light and completed their work early enough to allow them to walk back while there was still the last vestiges of daylight. They were as excited about the story emerging from Ivan's travels as he was, but this time they had a surprise awaiting them. Another vehicle parked in the yard, they knew Sonja's, but more people parked here at this time of the year was very unusual. Whoever they were, it would be good to meet as it got very dull with just the three of them.

The door burst open as Vlad and Piotr stamped the snow off their feet and entered the room.

They looked around, surprised to see so many new faces.

Once the introductions were over, any awkwardness evaporated as Korgai and the others listened to the exploits of the last few nights. Sonja understood now why Ivan had wanted to talk to her and regretted not being able to have a word in private earlier. But speaking to a trained shaman was a special occasion, and they planned on staying overnight. Sonja knew there would be some time when she could have a quiet word.

Korgai explained to all of them. "I don't know if you know, there are three shaman types. He assumed from the descriptions Ivan gave of how the shaman of old worked they were Por shamans, which meant they combined healing with rituals to evoke the spirits. He was also a Por. Ivan shook his head. He was only interested in the spirits. Korgai said that was Kam shamanism. There was yet another only involved in healing called Em shamanism.

He asked to see their drum and rattle. He shook his head and smiled. "You've done well to progress so far with these primitive tools. Wait a minute." He nodded to Mikhail, and they both returned to the fancy vehicle with armfuls of materials.

These they laid on the table. There were four circular wooden tubes about two and a half inches deep and thirteen inches across. There were also white, flat circles, about twenty-two inches wide, with holes punched around the edge and a big ball of thin, soft rawhide. It turned out this was all they needed to make a proper shamanic drum. The white circles were soft reindeer hide. Soon the three lads and Mikhail were busily creating their drums while Sonja and Zoya offered to make the beaters. These were sticks about twelve inches long, which needed binding with wadding and were finally covered with a thin wrapping of soft leather. They had to make sure there was enough over the edge to cut into a fringe, and they also bound the holding end with soft leather and had long thongs and attached beads and feathers.

In an hour, there was an impressive array of instruments ready for use.

Korgai said, "I suggest I do a ritual to cleanse and prepare these drums and beaters when we go to the cave. How about you and I go on a journey when we finish?" He looked at the others present and said, "All of you are welcome to come and observe the proceedings too."

The snow lay thick on the ground, and the trees looked like white ghosts as the party made their way carefully towards the cave. At the entrance, Korgai motioned for everyone to stop and wait while he and Ivan walked in and went towards the back to Ivan's usual place. Korgai's drum was bigger than the ones they had just made. He had decorated the front with a fierce-looking eagle, which Ivan thought looked like Korgai himself. The shaman sat cross-legged with the drum resting vertically on his thigh and started drumming a fast and relentless rhythm. The thrum made Ivan feel as if he was also vibrating. Then the shaman started a strange chant. It was just like those he had heard Guta and his father make. So, Ivan thought, this is how to summon the spirits. Korgai nodded to Ivan to close his eyes. Immediately he was soaring with that eagle, high in the clear blue sky. They swooped and flew complicated patterns, then returned to the earth, and Ivan heard the now-familiar four sharp beats. He was back in the cave, but what had they done? Where had they been? Why were they there at all?

Korgai explained. "When you're more experienced, you too could move through the upper and lower worlds. You've already developed considerable expertise in the lower world. But all practising shaman must find their spirit animal guardian and their spirit power animal. Let's do a special ritual to look for those tomorrow morning. Right now, we need to meet your people."

He allowed the others to come and make themselves comfortable. After they lit a small fire, Korgai threw some leaves on it. Soon the cave filled with pungent smoke. Again

Ivan recognised it as the same behaviour he had observed with Guta and his father.

Korgai swayed back and forth, muttering some sort of chant. He held each of the new drums and passed them through the smoke. He laid them down and did the same for the beaters. "There, I dedicated them to this work, and they're ready to labour on your behalf. Now they must meet you, so each person must move them through the smoke."

Excitedly, Vlad and Piotr held their drums and beaters over the fire to drench them with smoke. Then Ivor and Mikhail had to do the same. Once completed, Korgai nodded for all the men to follow his drumbeat, and when he stopped, they must continue until he told them to stop. As Korgai drummed, he swayed back and forward, just like Ivan had seen Guta doing. Slowly he added the chanting and nodded to Ivan to close his eyes and join him on their next journey.

One moment they were flying high in the sky, and the next, they were fish leaping in and out of the waves of an unknown sea. Like sea serpents, they dived deeper and deeper. Now Ivan recognised the familiar tunnels. At last, they arrived in the cave.

They observed the injured hunters beside the central hearth. Ivan saw it was easier for Kitam to care for them there as there was more room to move. Of the two with broken legs, one came from each cave. The man's wife from this cave was here to help care for him. Once the news reached the other cave, Ivan knew the wife would want to come too. However, the dazed one also came from the other cave. But he was unmarried. The local wife watched Kitam as she bathed her two patients and showed the woman what to do for her husband. When finished, Kitam administered more drops, which helped take the pain away and made them sleepy. They watched as Kitam sat beside and watched her two charges through the night. The three developed a fever during the night, but she could help with her drugs. Since the injuries were all visible and of known origin, there was no need for the intervention of the shaman.

Aiee was caring for Chen. Guta and his father were busy in the sacred cave. They performed the rituals to send the day's dead to the place of spirits. Korgai indicated to Ivan they would join them later, but for now, they watched the work of the medicine woman in the main cave. Kitam knew she had to sit and keep watch in case a spirit came to steal the life of one of her charges. When one of them, the one with internal injuries, groaned, she thought, "This might be the moment of death, but I can help him go comfortably." She was beside him and gave him more drops of the painkilling medicine. She watched as he soon drifted off to sleep again. She spoke in her head to the spirits. "Help me with this man. If you want him, allow him to come to you in his sleep. If it is your will, he stays with us show me this night and allow him to recover." She knew if destined to stay, he would survive the night. She watched him closely, frequently laying her hand on his forehead, brushing the hair away.

As the sky lightened and sent fingers of weak sunlight around the edges of the old Auroch curtain, Kitam looked at her patient again. His fever had gone, and now he breathed easily. She sighed with relief. The spirits had heard her prayer. She was sure now he would live, but it would take many days for him to heal. She doubted he could hunt again, but time would tell. The two with broken legs still had a fever, but not too severe. She piled furs on them to sweat out the badness.

Next, Ivan and Korgai watched the newly orphaned child, Chen, who was happy to spend the day with Aiee. But, by the evening, she wanted the attention of Guta. She knew better than to expect Kitam to pay her or anyone attention. She focussed solely on the care of her patients. Guta went to the other hearth and told Aiee he would take Chen.

As they moved to his hearth, Chen saw her parents one. Her loss hit her. The hearth was cold, with no one about it. That was where she had spent her short life. She gripped Guta's hand and dissolved into yet more sobs. He wondered how he could help, then reminded himself he was the storyteller. After lighting the fire, he sat by the hearth with her on his lap. Her head resting on his chest, he let her cry for a while, then, in a low voice, he talked.

He told her about her brave parents who had now gone hunting in the spirit world, but the spirits had given her a new home, and although they were old, she had new parents. He encouraged her to think about her parents and all the other hunters. To remember as they picked up their weapons and silently walked out of the cave. The beaters followed, carrying all the poles and leafy branches to make the barriers. He said, "You were sitting next to Inna and heard their footsteps go down the path into the early morning mist swirling about outside."

He softly spoke, "While that was happening here. The mammoths were making their way along the old paths they had walked before. They have excellent memories and live much longer lives than we do. We have to remember the pathway through the waters and sinking sands to travel safely to the Burda. They also remember the best feeding places and where to find water. Unfortunately, we did not know that one mammoth must have had the same thing happen before. She knew, and I expect she had lost her calf then. It made her furious because none of the mammoths or the people remembered her losing her calf. She would not allow it to happen again. We did a ritual, and the spirits showed us blood, which we thought meant there would be a good outcome for the hunt. Instead, we now know they were warning us of great danger."

Chen looked up at him. "So if they sent a warning, how come you got it wrong? It's because of you I've no parents." Tears were pouring down her little face. She sobbed as if her heart would break.

Guta felt so guilty. He, too, wanted to cry at the terrible loss of life. He supposed she was right. He tried to explain that the spirits did not use language like they were talking now, and nothing was easy to understand. Mostly they communicated in symbols, like the blood, which could be a warning of danger or a great success.

"I want to speak to these spirits. I want to tell them because they have taken my Amma and Adda, I have no one left in my life."

Guta swallowed, "Chen, that's not true. You have Kitam and me. We'll look after you; everyone in the clan loves you and will always see you are safe. Remember, Kitam delivered you and Inna as tiny babies. Maybe the spirit world thinks she is already like your mother. You have many people to look after you here, and the spirits needed hunters. None of us knows why some people are called to the spirit world when they are young, like your parents, while others live a long time and even want to go, but they cannot until the spirit world is ready for them."

"I want to speak to my parents to see if they are happy in the spirit world without me."

"Wait until you are full-grown before you speak with the spirits. But you can help me prepare their bones when the time is right. That will make them happy to know someone is here to look after their last needs."

She sat silent for a while, then sucking her thumb and clutching the rabbit skin doll, she nodded. She would do that, but he had to promise she could talk to her parents and the spirits when she grew up. He promised to give her the opportunity as soon as she was old enough.

Korgai lifted his hand. Vlad saw the gesture and beat the four sharp notes to call Ivan back from his travels.

Chapter 12

Ancient and modern communicate

Until he started his studies at the university, Ivan planned to work at the farm. He rose early, excited about travelling with Korgai, but now he had other responsibilities. He was busy in the barn when Sonja popped her head around.

He was concentrating on filling buckets with food for the sheep. Dust billowed around his head and settled on his hair and eyelashes.

"Hi Ivan, is it all right if I come and help you? Then we can talk."

He nodded his head, grinned and wiped a dusty forearm over his face. Ivan needed to talk to Sonja and get things straight in his mind, "Yes, come in. It'll be good to share the work. I promise I won't give you the messy jobs, though. It might spoil your shoes." Instead of her usual boots, she was still wearing her soft house shoes.

She grinned. "Should I change first?"

Shaking his head. "No, it'll be fine if you measure the food from the sacks into the buckets while I do all the running around." She was happy to oblige, knowing she would need to wash her face and hair later. Working like this, they could get the jobs done while Ivan talked. "Sonja, it was an awful experience. I know I'm only watching, it shouldn't affect me so much, but it did. My heart broke when I saw those mutilated bodies, the way the whole cave population, dwellers and visitors were so shocked and incapable of thinking, much less doing anything helpful." He shook his head. She saw he was still close to tears. "What broke me completely was the little girl left as an orphan. Guta was impressive. He was so matter-of-fact with her. No falseness, just reached out to her with love."

Sonja asked, "So, how did they sort things out?"

Ivan had a lop-sided smile. "Kitam. She didn't hesitate, examined all the injured, and prioritised who should be treated first. Plus bullying, in a gentle way, to get Guta and his father to not only prepare the dead but also provide leadership for the survivors."

"Did they not object to a woman doing this?"

Again Ivan stood still, buckets in hand, his sheep bleating loudly, wanting their food. "You know what, Sonja? We could learn a lot from these people. They are not obsessed like we are, who is the boss, males or females. They all work together like a well-oiled mechanism."

Sonja handed him another two buckets. "The food is getting low in this sack. Do we need another?"

He grinned. "No, I think that's everyone taken care of now."

He upended two buckets. "Do come and sit a moment. There will be no peace when we go inside."

They sat there staring into the sheep pens, and the sound of crunching provided the background as he went on. "Kitam is a quiet, efficient woman. They all needed that in their shocked state. Soon she had people scurrying about fetching water and heating it. Providing food and cutting more bracken to make beds."

Now they were quiet. He told her how impotent he felt. He could do nothing useful to help or comfort.

Finally, he sighed. "Sonja, I think it would be good to identify where the tragedy took place."

She pursed her lips. Thinking about how this lad's influence was changing her way of working, his experience was so real, his emotions intense. She nodded. "You know you have painted a realistic picture of the whole event. I think we should give it a try."

His tummy rumbled. Sonja laughed. "You poor starving guy, let's go inside."

They walked over to her truck first. "I've got a map book in the truck door. Let's grab that, then see if anywhere suggests itself."

When the rest of the party straggled into the kitchen, they found Sonja and Ivan pouring over a map. At that moment, the farmer's wife appeared and shooed them out so she could get on with cooking breakfast. The only other room big enough to accommodate them and the map was the floor in one dormitory. It was unusual as they all sat around the map while Sonja told them of Ivan's idea.

Korgai's eyebrows shot up, and he stroked his beard thoughtfully. "We need to get out and travel in spirit to feel where the tragedy happened, but I think it's an excellent idea. Ivan, do you think you could recognise the place again?"

Ivan nodded, "I'm sure if I see the valley, I'll be able to get my bearings."

They trailed into the kitchen. The aromas were enough to distract the most committed searcher of ancient hurts. The farmer's wife happily piled food onto their plates, but Korgai held up his hand. Delicious as it was, he knew they should not have too much to spirit travel. Ivan reluctantly agreed and waved yet another delicacy away. Mikhail, Zoya and Sonja were not restricted. Vlad and Piotr smelled the food and looked hungrily at the feast. Ivan saw the look and said, "Guys, come and help eat this feast. Korgai is miserable and says he and I must only eat a little. We have to do spirit travel." He pulled a face, but they could see his excitement at this new guy showing him a greater depth to his bumbling shamanism.

Soon the vehicles moved off with Sonja, Ivan, and Korgai in the lead while the others piled into Mikhail's vehicle. The snow and the poor roads meant the trucks could not go fast, yet Ivan's thoughts were ahead, going over all the times he had been on this road. Slowly Sonja swung left and moved onto the main road. Here the snow plough had cleared a path. Now there was snow piled up on the side of the road, but at least the way was clear, although she knew only too well how deceptive that could be with treacherous black ice ready to snatch at the wheels of an unwary driver.

Suddenly Ivan yelled, "Stop, stop. I'm sure this is the place where the beaters stood with their barriers."

Both vehicles pulled onto the side of the road. Standing around gazing at the changes thousands of years had made to the topography, Ivan had a niggling doubt. Then he recognised the main road headed through the valley was the same as where his 'people' had forced the herd to charge along. "I'm sure this is the place. Along there, about a quarter of a mile on the left is where the ravine branches off."

"Right, let's get going," Sonja called, jumping back into the relative warmth of the vehicle.

Excitedly Ivan pointed. "Look, Sonja, I'm right. It's there."

A narrow cleft led off to the left with a twisting path etched into its base, enticing them to follow it. While waiting for the others to arrive, the three jumped out and moved a little along. Korgai said, "Yes, I can still feel the emotions caught in the spirit world. Come, Ivan, we will need to go ahead with our drums."

The others, being scientists, were not sure this was the right way to approach the site of a massacre by a mammoth but kept quiet for the moment. After all, they were following in the footsteps of people a young lad had seen in a vision! They had to tamp down the pure scientist and see where this strange syncretic method might lead. They listened to the drumming of the shaman and his accomplice slowly growing fainter, not knowing what else they could do in terms of searching. Once again, they retreated into the warmth of the vehicles. Sonja started to worry as time passed. The knot in her stomach only eased when she saw Ivan come running along the path.

"Sonja, come, you've got to see this!" He looked wide-eyed and breathlessly said, "Yes, the rest of you can come too."

While the party trudged carefully along the path, avoiding little lumps of snow and ice. Sonja whispered to Ivan, "What's going on? What've you seen?"

Ivan smiled mysteriously, "Wait and see. It's worth waiting, I promise."

The undergrowth was short and stubbly here. They all saw Korgai standing in a slightly cleared area with his arms raised above his head, like a prophet of old, turning slowly around and chanting.

Ivan was bursting with excitement and pointed. "See that place there. One spearman died there. His spirit is telling Korgai all about it. This is what I saw when I followed them to the hunt."

Breathlessly Ivan reported the conversation he and Korgai had with the spirit. "The man was so scared he tried to scale the stone walls to avoid the angry cow. The calves were milling around, too, not knowing what to do. He slipped back down. He still tried to scrabble away. Although only calves, they were much bigger than he expected. In their panic, their feet crushed him."

Ivan took a deep breath and said, "Although Guta and his father were careful to do the ritual to send the spirits of the fallen back to the spirit world, this one was confused. He came back here instead. He's been waiting for someone to send him to the spirit world all this time. Whenever people come along the track, he pleads with them to release him, but they can't see him, only get a strange feeling which makes them shiver and want to run away. Korgai will release him back to the spirit world, but he told us about the hunting preparations. When Korgai comes back, he will describe it. If it matches what I saw in the cave, that will be validation, as Korgai knows nothing about my visions."

Sonja wanted to agree but decided it was best to say nothing.

Shortly after, Korgai joined the group standing around. He pointed out where each of the hunters had fallen, adding that the hunter he had spoken to confirmed everyone was so upset nobody at the time had thought to gather their weapons. Therefore, there was an excellent chance they might find the arrowheads and spearheads buried in the soil. They put markers where the spirit hunter had shown Korgai the positions they had laid in wait. After the cow had charged, nobody had stayed in place, all trying frantically to get away. Knowing all this, they should be able to work out where to look for these artefacts. Sonja felt on the firmer scientific ground and agreed they would put a few exploratory trenches in this spot in the spring.

Zoya's anxious voice called, "Guys, it's getting late. We need to be making our way back to the farmhouse."

Having guests thrilled the farmer's wife. To cater to them meant she banished everyone from her kitchen. Once again, they retired to the relative safety of the dormitory. Mikhail blinked behind his glasses. He found it so interesting how the different people and views came together. He was impressed to see the results of the cooperation between modern education and ancient traditions. Now they had to wait until the spring to see how accurate this relationship could be. He felt optimistic and wondered if a new branch of study might not open up in time to come.

"Guys, tomorrow morning, Zoya and I want to search the rock face for that food storage place and maybe the death rock too. Would anyone care to join us?"

Vlad, no longer awed by all these talented people, said, "If you don't mind waiting while we do our work with the animals first, Piotr and I would love to help."

Korgai shook his head, "No, I want to take Ivan on another journey, a quest one this time."

This meant Sonja was at a loose end. However, she decided it would be an excellent time to catch up on some work by writing a report on her laptop in the kitchen's warmth.

In the morning, they all gathered in the kitchen, where the beaming farmer's wife piled food onto their plates while discussing how things had turned out the day before.

Mikhail said, "This has been such a great time, so Zoya and I are returning to the cave. Ivan, can you describe what you saw when the men took food out of their stash."

Ivan gulped his coffee and said, "To be honest, I wasn't

paying too much attention to them at first. I saw the one guy leave the cave and turn right, not down the path but along the rock face. I thought that was an odd thing to do but wondered if they wanted to relieve themselves." He sat a moment staring inwardly and slowly sipping his coffee. "Then the first one knelt and felt along the rock for a bit. He appeared to pull and grunt. Next thing, a chunk of rock was lying next to him on the ledge, and he reached into a hole" he raised his shoulders and lifted his hands. "Well, I think it must have been another cave. His hand went quite a long way, and it looked like he felt for something. Next, I saw him pulling a bundle out of the hole." He tipped his head to one side and said, "I knew it was a chunk of meat. By now, the other chap had arrived and did the same thing, fished around and drew out more meat. I thought how smart it must be, like having a deep freeze. They both pushed and shoved the rock back into place before returning to the cave."

Mikhail looked speculatively, then nodded. "Sonja, how deep are the layers from the present floor of the cave to the very deepest?"

Sonja thought a moment, then said, "It depends on where in the cave you want to measure, but on the whole, I would think about four feet."

He looked at Zoya, "That's from all the debris of living, but how much do you think stuff will have piled up outside?"

As usual, when she thought, she ran her hands through her hair. She said, "Ivan says they walked along a ledge, so with any luck, if we can find the vestiges of a ledge, it shouldn't be too much. If not, stuff that's blown there might have accumulated at the same rate as the debris inside. In that case, I doubt we could find it just with a visual inspection."

Sonja looked puzzled, "What other kinds of inspection could you do?"

Smirking, Zoya said, "You guys do need to move with the times. Geophysics could detect a cave in the rock face. Especially if we roughly knew the vicinity. And we do from Ivan's description."

Ivan looked excited. "Then we could also look for the ritual cave the same way. But I only know it is somewhere at the back of the South Chamber."

Korgai interjected. "We will do a ritual in the cave this morning to find Ivan's guardian animal and his power one. Then we'll follow the old shamans to their cave. I want to talk to them, and when we return, we can check out where it is in relation to the main living spaces."

First, the three lads all had their work to do. Mikhail was happy to give Vlad and Piotr a lift to the other farm and wait for them while Sonja and Zoya assisted Ivan. Korgai said he wanted to sit and think to prepare correctly for the vital ritual he needed to do with Ivan.

A few hours later, Korgai and Ivan again made their way to the cave laden with their drums, blankets, and the stuff to make a fire. For this occasion, Korgai dressed in his shamanic clothing as it was only polite to wear the correct costume when visiting other shamans, even if the others were thousands of years ago.

It was dim at the back of the cave, but they were comfortably settled, and the little fire cracked in the hearth they had created. Korgai again sprinkled herbs from a pouch hanging from his belt. Together they drummed. By now, Ivan could move into that altered state of shamanic consciousness quickly and easily. He saw the mound and the hole as usual, but then an eagle swooped down and forced him to look up. He felt himself move off with the eagle as a companion. Once again, they soared in blue skies so different from the bruised purple and green coloured sky with snow threatening outside.

As they moved through this spirit landscape, Ivan saw a stag stand and stare at them. His rack of antlers is a magnificent branching work of art. The stag then took off, leaping and running so fast it was like a brown streak moving over the green grass. As suddenly as it had taken off, it stopped and dropped its head, calmly cropping verdant pasture. Once again, it raised its head and looked at them, then turned to look away to the right. The eagle Korgai flew down with Ivan following. They spoke to this magnificent stag. It was Ivan's guardian animal and had been waiting for him to acknowledge its presence. From now on, wherever Ivan travelled in the spirit world, this magnificent creature would be with him. Running and leaping while protecting and guiding him into safe ways. Ivan felt tears prickle in his eyes to have such a magnificent creature as this for a guardian. It made him not only emotional but confused. He always thought of himself as a very ordinary guy, only to discover his protector was such an impressive creature.

As they journeyed on, a strange combination of fierce eagle and swift, alert stag, they saw a little squirrel. This curious creature ran around Ivan, stopped to look at him, and then disappeared up a tree before sitting in front of him again. Korgai told Ivan to reach out, take hold of the little creature, and bring it back. Once they were back in the cave, Korgai spoke. "Little squirrel, take up your place in his chest. Stay by his heart. This is your forever place." The shadowy creature jumped into Ivan while Korgai pressed a hand on the centre of Ivan's chest. Ivan expected it to hurt. Instead, he experienced a warm feeling near his heart.

"Korgai, what happened there? I felt a tug on my chest, and now I feel a warm pulsing sensation over my heart."

"You will feel that each time you add a power animal. As time passes, you will need to add animals to help you deal with complex situations."

After the ritual, Korgai said, "Ivan, you now have protection and power. The stag is your guardian spirit animal. The squirrel is the first of what could become many spirit-power animals. You are now on the path to being a powerful Kam shaman."

Ivan blinked back the emotional response. His heart was racing. So many things had happened in such a short space of time. He sat reviewing the most recent events before joining the others, inspecting the rock face. Meanwhile, Korgai journeyed back to join the shamans of old.

Korgai joined Guta and his father at the back of the cave near the seeing cave. They looked surprised as they gazed at this new shaman, a spirit one come to join them. They were flattered by this new visitor and invited him to join them in their ritual space. They entered in the same manner as usual but with heavy hearts. They lit a fire using the tiny bow drill, which Guta was now an expert at using. Korgai indicated he was impressed with this skill. Once the lazy tendrils of smoke wreathed their way up, the older man sprinkled the dried herbs. Soon the whole place was a pungent mixture of smoke and smell. They mixed the pigments and carefully recorded the tragic events of the hunt.

The spirits beyond the rock face and the cave's surfaces directed their strokes. The cow mammoth appeared to be bursting out of a protuberant rock surface. They showed only her head and massive tusks. The rest of her powerful body they knew was the other side of the thin membrane of the cave wall. Once the recording was complete, they sat again on the floor and rocked and chanted, waiting to reach the spirit world. Once there, they met another human like them. They spoke of their guilt, thinking the blood was a good omen, not a warning. Between the three, they talked and waited until a spirit helper appeared and told them the hunt was, in fact, a great success. They needed the hunters in the spirit world while Guta and Kitam had their longed-for child. Korgai told them about Ivan's visits. They confirmed they had not seen him, but they knew there was another presence and welcomed him. Guta told Korgai he felt a strong tie to the young man as if they were kin.

Korgai returned to the present while the other two returned to their time to report the outcome to Kitam. She pointed out it was not up to them to know how the spirits worked. They were responsible for sending those who had died back to that world. And for them to rejoice in the beautiful gift of the child.

Chapter 13

Thread Making

Early Spring

Ivan was bored. He looked around for something to do. He was at a loose end for the first time in his life. The yard felt empty after the visitors left and Vlad returned to work. Piotr had been appointed as the official shepherd. He was sensitive to Ivan's feelings, having cared for the flock for many years. As the new guy, he decided changes could wait until Ivan moved to the city. Instead, he took the sheep out for an early-season wander around the pastures. He did not plan to stay long anywhere but to get the feeling of being the authentic shepherd. He had helped out frequently, but now they were his flock. He could decide where to go and for how long to stay out. He knew he would have to supplement their feed on his return, but it would be good for the flock and him to enjoy the weak sunlight, check out the budding trees and grasses, and revel in being employed in a real job. After all, he, too, had joined the ranks of school leavers. Unlike his brother and Ivan, he had been allowed to finish high school, which he appreciated since his brother's sacrifice got him here. Now he wanted to earn and somehow pay him back. They had talked about it. "Vlad, now I'm earning a regular salary. Can't we find somewhere to live in better circumstances?"

Vlad shook his head. "No, not yet. But I feel something will come of this cave of Ivan's. I feel as attached to those ancient spirit people as he does. Although I don't get to see them, I help him reach the right places. Also, his descriptions make them feel alive, almost as if they live in the next valley."

They were sitting in their tiny bedroom with blankets to keep them warm when Piotr smiled and said, "Do you think I'll be able to move into Ivan's old room?"

Vlad threw his head back and laughed. "Not a chance. He will still be at the farmhouse on vacations and any other time if Sonja needs him to do something special. The farmer's wife gave him that table as a desk plus the heater. You could ask to use the heater when he's not there. One would be good in here too."

Piotr looked thoughtful. "You know what I'm going to do with my first pay packet?"

Vlad quipped. "Waste it on rubbish just for the fun of spending."

His brother looked offended and then punched Vlad on the arm. "No, nothing like that, you idiot. I was going to ask Ivan to bring you a heater."

Vlad dropped his head and looked ashamed. "Sorry, bro, I wasn't being nasty. I said the first thing which came into my head."

Piotr snorted. "You expect me to believe you? Stop thinking I'm still a kid! Believe it or not, I'm very thankful for all you've done for me and wanted to make a small gesture to show my gratitude."

Softly, Vlad muttered, "You don't owe me anything. You always shared your books and lessons, so we both got an education. Two for the price of one!"

* * *

On one of their frequent phone calls, Ivan asked, "Sonja, when you come up next time would you mind buying a few small presents? I want to give my Mum and the girls a little something to remember me while I'm away."

Sonja laughed. "Ivan, you are crazy. You won't be far away and will be stationed back at the farmhouse during the university vacations. Yes, I'll get a few things for you."

When she rattled into the yard, she had gone to town and bought armfuls of trinkets, which the salesman had assured her were all the rage for young girls.

Ivan felt concerned. "Sonja, these are so lovely, and the girls will love them, but how will I pay you back? I'm not looking after the sheep anymore. I am jobless and penniless."

Sonja smiled. "You're a nitwit. Last time you came into town with me, don't you remember we started a bank account for you? I also told you if you passed your exams, I could employ you to supervise the exploration of the caves. You've passed! Now you're on my payroll. You have done more than oversee the work. You have opened up so many new avenues for us to explore. Your salary has been going into your bank account. You have more than enough to cover the cost of these few things. Now, how are you getting to your parents?"

He blinked. "I didn't know all this had happened. Thank you so much. I'll walk to the end of the road and catch the bus to go home."

Sonja shook her head. "No, I'll give you a lift there and back. I want to meet your family; you've met my parents, so it's only right I meet yours. Anyway, it's time I saw that sheep, sorry ram of yours too. I need to tell the farmer's wife I'll stay for a few days. Then you must return to town with me as Mikhail has organised a little surprise. Then you move in with my parents, ready to start your new life."

They bumped down the farm track towards the main road and set off towards Ivan's parents' place. He showed her where to park and loaded up the parcels. They set off down the rocky path. Bone knew they were there long before anyone else and came running over. He was so big and strong now when he head-butted Ivan, all the parcels went flying. That brought the girls out, dancing ahead of the visitors swinging parcels.

Calling out in unison, "Mama, look who's come home."

Ivan's mother hurried to the door and saw a strange sight, Ivan, an older woman carrying parcels and the big ram happily trotting at their heels.

"Come in, come in," she hurriedly scooped toys off the chairs for her visitors.

It embarrassed Ivan how poor his home looked compared to Sonja's parent's beautiful house.

But she did not notice. She just dropped the parcels onto the chair and stuck her hand out. "Hi, I'm Sonja, Ivan's friend and employer!"

Ivan's Mum looked confused. I thought he would study at the university. How can you employ him too? We are pleased he's going to university, but we have been worried about how we'll cope without his financial help."

Ivan stepped in and explained they would get more now as Sonja wanted him to work while he studied, so she did not need to worry.

Soon they were all chatting. The girls squealed with delight at their presents. His Mum asked about his other big parcel. He explained he had been working with an authentic shaman who had shown him how to make his drum, which he had brought to show her. He drew it out of its bag. She stood looking at it, tears rolling down her face. The girls now sat around him as he drummed for them. Sonja noticed his Mum still had a tear in her eye.

"That's like the drum the old man played when I was a child. I wonder if he was also a shaman. Wait here. I have something for you."

She disappeared for a short time into her room and returned with two little bundles.

"That old man gave me these when I married and left the village. As he handed them to me, he said something strange. I was to look after them carefully. One day I would know who to give them to so they could carry on their work. I kept them on my little shrine. I knew they were sacred but did not understand. Now I think I do. His drumming and yours are the same. I assume he must have been the shaman. The government banned these practices in those days. The government officials could punish you if they got to know. Now it's all very different, though. I have looked after them all these years, but now they're yours."

He looked in the two little pouches, just like the ones Korgai had hanging off his belt. One was empty but had a herby smell. He presumed this was the one for the dried herbs to sprinkle on the fire. The other had a beautiful quartz crystal, clear but for a little smudge of green caught in its stony depths. He could feel the power just by touching it.

There were tears in his eyes as he hugged his mother. This was her way of saying she was happy with his chosen path. Sonja looked on and carefully wiped a tear away when the girls burst into the room again.

The older one said, "Ivan, we've been saving things from when we go out walking. Now we want you to have them.

Can you put them on your drum?"

Each girl stepped up, and in the palms of their hands was a selection of bird feathers. He smiled. "These are just right. I'll put them onto the beater, not the drum; otherwise, I might squash them."

They giggled happily. So long as their big brother had something from them, they were happy.

Ivan's dad appeared then, surprised to see they had visitors. Soon he was telling Ivan about the nucleus of his new flock. He kept a note of all the ewes he put with Bone. Now he had two ewes, as they had discussed before. Bone stuck his head in the door as if to say, "They are my harem, keep your hands off them."

After eating a simple meal, Sonja and Ivan returned to the vehicle, accompanied part of the way by Bone, and drove back to the farmhouse. There was still enough time for Ivan to visit the cave. Sonja offered to do the drumming in place of Vlad. She wanted to feel part of this journey, which, after all, only started because of her giving Ivan those books.

This time, as Ivan went into his shamanic state of consciousness, he saw his stag. This was such a different way to travel. In his mind, he told the animal he wanted to go to the original cave community.

Without feeling as if he were moving through tunnels or tubes, he was aware of being with the clan. They were at their summer camp. He walked unseen with Kitam and the two girls, Chen and Inna. They were laughing and talking while they were out foraging. Suddenly Kitan stopped and gazed into a large, muddy ditch. The girls saw and asked, "What is it, Kitam?"

Kitam became quite excited. "I've not noticed this here before, but there were ditches of it where I grew up."

"Would you like us to pick it for you?"

She nodded as the girls happily jumped into the mud to haul armfuls of long muddy white fibres out of the water. They piled it into a collecting basket. Once back at the tents, she carefully hung them out to dry.

Ivan was back at the cave without being aware of the passing of time. A deep red sun hung just above the edge of the ravine. It caught the gold and red of the leaves as they started to flutter towards the ground. It was late autumn. There was a long trail of silent people who trod steadily along the narrow valley, the home stretch. Little clouds of dust kicked up by their feet. The horses, equally weary, dragged the sledges. Piled high with stuff the clan would need over the winter. The frequent visits by the hunters with meat and other foodstuffs for their larder meant they knew the cave was safe from intruders.

This return was no different to other times until the girls carried the baskets with the white threads and dumped them at Kitam's hearth. At this strange addition, Aiee took notice. The threads intrigued her. "Kitam, what is that stuff you have brought back? Is it a new medicine? How is it used?"

Kitam laughed. "These have no healing properties in the medicine way of thinking, but when I have dyed them, they can decorate clothing."

Aiee's eyebrows rose. "What do you mean, dye?"

Kitam explained. "It's a way of putting colour into them by using plants and things by heating them in water."

Pulling her mouth into a lop-sided look with a faraway look, she patted them. "I think I'd better make you some baskets just for that; otherwise, you might change the taste of the food or water. I've had a good grass year and collected extra. Now I know why."

It touched Kitam. "Thank you, Aiee, that would be wonderful. Could I put the design on Inna's tunic too? Then, as usual, the girls will match. I saw the pattern in a dream. They will be the most beautiful swan maidens anyone has ever seen. I have some white beads too."

Ivan watched alongside the other women as Kitam dipped the threads into different baskets full of hot water and strange ingredients like ground-up roots, handfuls of leaves, and scrapings of lichen. After a reasonable time of heating the water, she pulled them out, rinsed everything in cold water, and then hung each bundle of colours up to dry near the fire. The threads had taken the colour well. There was red, many shades of green, yellow, purple and dusky pink. To achieve all these colours and shades, she had used things the others would not have considered, an advantage of being a medicine woman and knowing the properties of different plants.

Odo was the best at knapping and pressure flaking and using the bow drill with a long fine point. Kitam had found the long bones of several birds and explained. "Odo. I want to make a needle with a tiny hole drilled into it to stitch the tunics together and apply the coloured threads and beads to the girl's tunics."

He looked confused for a moment. "What's wrong with the awl everyone else uses?"

Smiling, she continued. "The awl is fine to make the holes in the clothing and to use rawhide to stitch them together, but it is too thick for this fine thread I have prepared."

Still, with a scowl on his face, he growled. "Show me the stuff you want to use."

Obediently, she returned to her hearth and picked up a basket of coloured fibres.

Lifting a handful of the thin filaments out of the basket,

he marvelled. "How did you make this so fine? What grows with these colours, anyway?"

Smiling, she replied. "I didn't make the thread. It grows like that, but I dyed it using different plants."

Full of admiration for this talented woman, he returned the thread to the basket and murmured. "I'll see what I can do. If it works, could you give some to my wife to decorate our daughter's tunic too?"

Soon she had a beautiful long bone needle with a hole just the right size for the thread. Sitting on her favourite tree stump made comfy, covered with a thick pelt. She looked like a Queen surrounded by tributes. Spread around her were all the things she would need to finish the tunics for Chen and Inna.

Unlike Guta going into a trance, she had seen the design she wanted to create in a dream.

Kneeling on the ground using a tiny piece of charcoal saved from her hearth fire, she marked the design onto the soft doeskin tunics she stitched in the summer.

The design showed a string of swans flying from right to left on Chen's tunic and in the opposite direction on Inna's across the front of their tunics.

Using the newly created coloured threads, she picked out a forest design with green trees, coloured flowers and rich brown earth. The all-important swans were embellished with the tiny white beads left from her mother-in-law's pouch.

She carefully marked where she wanted to stitch with a tiny piece of charcoal saved from the fire. She had seen the pattern in a dream. She would make a string of swans flying from right to left on Chen's garment and another from left to right on Inna's across the front of their tunics. She planned to pick out the pattern of a forest scene in different colours, green trees, colourful flowers and rich brown earth. The all-important birds were embellished with the tiny white beads still in her mother-in-law's pouch.

The result of her handiwork was so striking there was a clamour from the other mothers whose daughters were also going through their swan maiden ceremonies at the next summer camp. They kept Odo busy making needles for all of them while the trade for the thread was brisk. The two girls had white swan designs thanks to the old lady's white bead stash. Kitam made a point of saving some thread and needles to swap at the next Burda for more beads. She knew how to make them but was unsure she had the time or patience to do so.

Kitam was glad Guta did not want his top decorated. However, while she was busy with this handwork, she carefully carried out his black feather cloak. Guta had inherited it from his father, who, in turn, had it from his father, and so on back so long no one could remember a time when it was new.

They rushed to collect it whenever Kitam or the girls saw a black feather. Better, though, if they chanced to see a dead raven or crow, they always made sure they gathered as many long black feathers as possible since the cloak always seemed to need repairs, and it was bad luck to kill one of these birds. While Kitam was about this decorative work, she checked the talon necklace he was required to wear for ritual work. This was a scary-looking item again passed down from shaman to shaman. It comprised soft twisted thongs of rawhide with eagle's talons attached.

Meanwhile, Guta was beside Odo, both absorbed in an unusual activity. On the ground was a beautiful green stone that Odo had knocked off a bigger chunk lying beside them. Now he was using his bow drill. Back and forth his hand went, slowly making a hole in the stone. As Ivan watched, it became apparent that they were making a bead. He wondered if they were trying to replace the one Guta had buried with his son. It was slow, laborious work, bow for a bit, then Guta needed to drop a little water on the stone, and the process went again.

At last, there was a stone with a hole. It was still a long way off being a bead, though. By watching this, Ivan could tell Sonja how they made the holes, but he would need to return many times more to watch how they finally formed it into a bead.

Chapter 14

In the Tundra

Sofia Sokolov was in her element again with another young person to cater for and chat with after work. After their evening meal, she said, "Maksim, how do you feel about having Ivan lodge here? I am delighted to have someone who might appreciate my cooking. You and Sonja were never the best, and all you both want to do is talk about the latest scientific papers you've read. I hope to be able to talk at dinner about more interesting subjects."

"Yes, dear, but remember, he will be pushed to the limit studying. Please don't make him feel inferior. Remember, he has only ever lived on a farm and worked as a shepherd. He's not likely to have a clue about everything you want to talk about, and his head is full of that other activity with a drum. What's it called?"

She sighed. "It's called shamanism. I think it's so fascinating. It's like time travelling. Which reminds me, I must get a few books on time travel for him to read."

The prof refilled his pipe and replaced it in his pocket. He knew better than to light it in the dining room, but it kept his fingers busy. He was only permitted to smoke in his study, his quiet personal retreat from his dynamic wife and her social life. His study was a reflection of his personality. His desk was covered in an untidy mess of notes and scientific papers crouched in the corner of the room, looking like a trapped animal. From the door, a quick look around, you would know his favourite place, the saggy old leather armchair with a view out the window onto a neat garden beside the fire. In his mind, the best of anything he could want was light and warmth, surrounded by books, since the walls were covered in shelves housing his extensive library.

When spring finally arrived in the mountains, Ivan had moved into the Sokolov's house and was deeply immersed in his studies and enjoying every minute.

Sophia said, "Ivan, we thought you might like the bedroom where you stayed before. As you know, it's at the other end of the house from ours. I thought it would give all of us privacy."

Ivan breathed a sigh of relief. He could continue his shamanic drumming and exercises. Even better, he discovered he could still visit the people in "his" cave in spirit without needing to be there physically. He should have known that the spirit world had different boundaries than his physical one.

Ivan was the epitome of a diligent student. He knew he had to prove he deserved his place here. He tried never to miss a lecture or a tutorial except for Yegor's tutorials. At his first attendance, Yegor had sneered. "Ah, so the caveman has deigned to attend. What discoveries have you made now? Or rather, what have you planted at the site now?"

Some students, unaware of the undercurrent, were shocked at their lecturer's insinuations. Another one snickered until Yegor scowled at her, "What's so funny young lady?"

She gulped and lowered her eyes. Incensed, Ivan decided not to reply. He was too upset to take part in any discussion, though. After classes, he strode back to his lodgings, went into his room and drummed, not to go into an altered state but to release the anger he felt roiling in his stomach.

Sonja's dad hammered on the door. "Ivan, are you joining us for dinner? It's all ready and there is someone here to see you."

He stored his drum in its case, washed his face and flicked a comb through his hair before going along the passage to the dining room. He felt like a little boy. A thought flittered through his mind. Should he move into university accommodation? The practical side of his mind kicked in. There, he would have to pay for the room and then pay for food in the canteen or get his own. He knew that would cost much more than the Solokovs suggested as bed and board. The responsibility to send money home was still there. He couldn't afford to give in to a whim. He tamped down his bad mood. Who was this person waiting to see him? After the day he had experienced, the last thing was someone asking about shamanism

He slunk into the room, still distressed. He did not look up, only mumbled. "I'm sorry I did not hear you calling earlier."

Prof Sokolov smiled. "I surmise something happened today to upset you. Maybe you should tell Sonja."

He shook his head, eyes still downcast. He gripped the back of the chair and said, "No, I can fight my own battles, thank you."

"Yes, you can normally, but now you should tell me, and right now. I presume it was something to do with our friend Yegor Morozov? I need to know exactly what it was."

Ivan's head shot up. Sitting at the table opposite him was

Sonja.

His face went red, then paled alarmingly. "Ivan, are you all right?" called Sonja as she rose from her chair and hurried around the table. She guided him into the chair as Sophia Sokolov walked into the room carrying a pot of stew. Looking at her mother, she said, "First, you need some food. Then we'll talk."

He scowled and looked mutinous but realised he had no escape. He had to tell Sonja and her parents what had happened. Sonja nodded her head. "That's what I heard from Katina. She came to request a transfer from Yegor's tutorial group. She said she could not be with someone who belittled another, much less a student. I assumed it was you. I came over after work and decided to let you work off your anger. Let's eat, and then we can see what to do."

Sofia Sokolov was happy Sonja had arrived and could sort the problem out, but only after they had eaten. She would be upset if they neglected the food she had prepared.

Shamanically, Ivan went back to his people at least weekly, sometimes more frequently, and he observed their everyday activities. On one visit, he saw how they stored their water. It took him a while to work it out. They cleaned animal stomachs to hang up, filled with water. They had to haul it from the river, which meandered through the valley below the cave. A convenient rock jutted into the running water, so they always had clean, fresh water, not that which swirled around in eddies along the bank, collecting silt and leaves. He saw each hearth had its water skin and a few baskets for heating water beside it.

On one occasion months later, Ivan observed people going out to the communal larder. Every time someone went out, he looked carefully to see if he saw any distinguishing marks within the environment. One day, he was fortunate enough to see a group of men and a horse pulling a chunk of ice on a sledge. This fascinated him for two reasons. Firstly, this was the same vehicle the horses' dragged to the Burda. Secondly, they were using it at the cave site. They moved two rocks out of the storeroom entrance as he peered over their shoulders. One man crawled in and passed out the remaining foodstuffs. Ivan could see it was not just meat but tubers and other vegetable matter.

Once they were happy, the store was empty. They brought the ice block close. It was too big to fit through the entrance. However, a few hard blows from a great chunk of rock had it split into sizes that suited them. He watched wide-eyed as they carefully lined the whole space with ice before packing the food again. It seemed the area on the left was for meat and the right for vegetable matter. Once completed and the foodstuff stowed away with the rocks to seal the entrance, the men smiled and nodded at each other, a job well done.

Next, they turned their attention to the transport. Ivan observed them take the sledge apart. They tied the wooden struts and sliders together with rawhide. The skins comprising the body folded easily. They stored the entire vehicle in the cave, which did not take up much room. Ivan looked to see where they stowed it. Since it was of organic matter, there would be little evidence of it in the current trenches. But it would be helpful to know more about how the different parts of the cave served the inhabitants.

The next day, he burst into Sonja's office, "Sonja, I've seen how they make their deep freeze!"

She looked confused for a moment, "How? Who uses their deep freeze?" As soon as the words were out of her mouth, she knew that was a silly thing to say. Ivan would only be as excited as this by another glimpse into "his people's" lives.

He drew her pictures of what he had seen, how they

stacked the ice and lined every surface. She looked thoughtful. They both longed to identify this storage cave. This led to another topic, "Ivan, I think it's time we opened up a trench at the mammoth massacre site, don't you? I've got a new contingent of students arriving in two weeks when the season opens. Would you be prepared to take charge down there?"

He smiled delightedly. It would mean working out in the open, and they could get a digger there. "Vlad has done well protecting the cave through the winter. Could I get him or Piotr to drive the digger? It would help supplement their incomes."

They poured over maps and drew lines, joining the dots where the spirit hunter had told Korgai their positions just before the mayhem started. Using computer generation software, they were able to feed in the known locations of the hunters and then tried to follow the possible movements of the mammoth cow. The calves' movements would have been random, but they also knew the exact spot their hunter died, which helped work out what happened.

Soon the printer spewed pages of lines and squiggles from the information fed into the program. They decided on where to site the trenches. Sonja felt odd to be working in what she would have up to now termed a non-scientific manner, yet with the computer program, she could see the positions were possible. She knew it was a risk. Only once the trenches were dug would they know if this was an acceptable approach to adopt.

Weeks later, Piotr drove the digger and made the trenches where Ivan had pegged them out. Then the team jumped down and started scraping away. They made their first find—a perfect stone spear point in no time. Overjoyed, Ivan saw the results were phenomenal. During the dig, they made finds at about every place Sonja and Ivan had plotted and expected. All were weapons, spear points at the end of the ravine and arrowheads when they moved towards the opening of the gully. This fitted with the scene Ivan had witnessed and the report the spirit hunter gave to Korgai. Now Sonja had to accept there was something in Ivan's unorthodox way of working.

Not everyone was happy with the increased success rate or the unusual collection methods. Yagor pointedly referred to Ivan as 'The Caveman' in front of all the other students. He also consistently marked Ivan's written work down. He said, "How can I be expected to read this childish illiterate scrawl? Also, I don't believe this sudden rash of discoveries is authentic. He probably made them himself and planted them wherever he felt."

These were serious accusations. Consequently, Sonja agreed for the lab to send the finds to an independent laboratory in Finland. Interestingly, the dates of all the discoveries falling within the mammoth hunt's time limits were verified. That shut the insufferable man up for a short time before he came up with more accusations.

Ivan was nearing the end of his studies, but this unpleasantness, the baiting and the accusations made him want to give it all up. Mikhail came round to the house, "Hi my friend, what's going on? I heard about you wanting to throw in the towel. Sonja is a dyed-in-the-wool scientist; for her to accept what you have done and proved right is a real game-changer. We all believe in you and your unorthodox methods. You can't just give up because one person is a bastard. We believe in you. We want you to carry on. The profession is so rigid and dominated by a few powerful personalities that it's time to break it down. Keep on. We're with you all the way."

They sat and talked until late at night, and then Mikhail threw in the final titbit. "I've heard from Korgai. He wants to know if you would come and stay with him for a few weeks."

It touched Ivan. His friends believed in him and backed him, then this invitation. "I'd like to go, but I need to clear it with Sonja first."

Mikhail replied, "Of course, let's go and see her in the morning."

Sonja was in her office when they came in. Mikhail had not seen her for a few weeks, "Sonja, you look exhausted. What's wrong?"

She smiled, "Nothing is wrong. I'm tired, that's all."

She looked at the schedules for student supervision at the cave, "Ivan, do you think Vlad can cover for you?"

Ivan knew Vlad would be glad for the extra work. The money he earned looking after the site in the winter made a big difference in his life as he saved to marry.

"He would bite my hand off to do that work, so don't worry. But do you mind if I go?"

She shook her head, "It's a great opportunity. Go for it."

The little plane came to land, using its skies instead of wheels. All Ivan could see was white. Snow and ice on the ground, and grey-white clouds above. He walked carefully to the little shack, the air terminal, the control tower, and anything else anyone wanted it to be. Waiting in there was Korgai, "Welcome, Ivan, good to see you again after all these years. We'll go to my house, then decide what to do."

Another first, waiting outside, was a team of sleigh dogs. Their bright red traces were trailing at their feet. Ivan looked at them and back to Korgai, "Is this the Siberian Uber service?"

Korgai laughed, "Too much snow and ice for vehicles

here. Yes, this is the way I move around. My Laika dogs are a better option than mechanical transport."

Ivan liked the look of these dogs. They were all colours, mostly white, with swaths of black and brown. One of the lead dogs had a white head, but two black fur patches around its icy blue eyes stared back at him. They had such a thick coat they could easily withstand the low temperatures. He thought growing up in the mountains was cold, but these temperatures were in another league.

Korgai was pleased he liked the dogs, "Come, get on, stand beside me. You can see more that way. All my family has dogs like these. We northern Yugur use them for herding. Tomorrow you will come with me and see my reindeer."

They stayed in a small, snug hut, drinking and talking until late. Korgai gave him the typical clothing of the people. Ivan shook his head to refuse, "It's fine. I brought some warm clothing with me."

Korgai chuckled, "Yes, I can see, and it's okay for you in your mountains, but it gets much colder here. It can go to minus 30, but it's warmer this time of the year. You will wear the same as all of us. Reindeer hide is the answer to the cold. You can take the outfit back with you too. I think maybe your ancient cave people dressed like us. It's the only way to survive. Next time you travel, look carefully at their clothing. I know none of it will have survived, but wearing this and seeing them, you will have a better idea."

It was still dark, although there was a tinge of light when Korgai woke Ivan. "Today, we'll check on my herd. The dogs are waiting. We'll stop for food on the way."

Dressed appropriately, they were soon flying over the snowy landscape. Unlike the day before now, there was a vast blue expanse above. Then Ivan saw a tiny dot far above. He pointed and said, "Is that an eagle?"

Korgai chuckled, "Yes, it's a real one, but as you know, it's also my spirit guide. That means we will have a successful day. It worried me yesterday thinking bad weather might blow in before we could get out there."

The dogs were indefatigable, running straight and true. They knew where to go without urging with their incredible sense of smell and direction. Hours later, as Ivan felt he could not stand much longer, they made a wide turn to the right, heading for a copse of straggling trees. Snuggled in the centre was a log cabin, smoke curling lazily up into the sky.

"We stop here for a short time. My sister lives here with her son. He goes out to supervise the herders if I am away or working. In the winter, all of us, plus the dogs, bring the animals closer to home so we can supplement their feed. I'm pleased to see you have your drum with you. We will need it soon, and you can thank the herd for their help since that hide came from them, given freely."

Korgai's sister laid out a feast on her little table. She smiled shyly at Ivan and waved her hand for him to help himself. He was about to refuse, but the tantalising aromas broke his hesitation. Soon both his plate and Korgai's resembled mini mountains. With a mouthful of food, Korgai said, "Elder sister thinks she must feed everyone who steps through her door. She's been like this since she took the elder woman position after our mother died. It's time for us to go, though. I'm not sure the dogs will appreciate the extra weight!"

The dogs had been lolling on the ground waiting, but as the men stepped out, they leapt up and showed every sign of enjoying their journey. Their destination was a vast snow plain where the reindeer roamed, scratching up the snow.

Ivan asked, "What are they eating? I can't see any grass

here."

Korgai replied. "They are eating what you call Reindeer moss, which is a lichen." Korgai went on. "These animals are so well adapted to this white light they can see things we can't. For instance, they see arctic hares or wolves as dark shadows because they see the reflection of ultraviolet light. When it comes to wolves, that's how they can avoid them if the pack try to creep up and kill one."

Ivan thought he saw a dark smudge in the distance. He blinked and pointed. "Korgai, what is that over there?"

Laconically Korgai said, "That's our destination."

They pulled into a small settlement, about six conical tents made of larch poles, like the trees around the log cabin. Ivan recognised the Reindeer skins attached to the poles.

Korgai saw him looking and said, "In the warm weather, we would use birch bark attached to the tent poles as tents. The rest of the year, we use deerskin as it is a better insulator." Ivan discovered to his horror, that there was so little wood they only lit the fire to cook, but since he was visiting, they made an exception.

After a simple meal cooked by one of his relatives, Korgai pulled out his drum and signalled to Ivor to do the same. Everyone in the tent silently left to gather elsewhere while Korgai sprinkled the herbs on the little fire. The two went journeying as the smoke swirled around their heads, then snaked up to the small hole in the tent skin above them.

First, Korgai's eagle met Ivan's stag. Then they moved off, looking for more power animals for Ivan. Korgai said, "You know Ivan, you have the power to become a healer shaman."

Ivan's eyes widened, and then he shook his head and said

emphatically. "No, whatever you say, I'm only interested in helping the spirits from the cave. I want to be able to talk to them. I don't ever want to do healing work."

Korgai looked disappointed but said, "Whatever path you wish to follow is your choice."

Soon their journey took them to Ivan's haunt. As they joined the cave folk, they again saw it was late autumn. The late afternoon light was already fading as the horses' sides heaved, snorting and blowing as they dragged the poles and the hides for the tents. Meanwhile, the adults followed, walking slowly up the incline. Laden, with baskets and bags, they wearily trudged up the long narrow path leading to their home cave. The younger children still had energy and ran ahead, yelling with excitement. They wanted to explore their hearths and ensure no wild animals had been in while everyone was away. Although the hunters frequently checked, the children hoped for even more excitement.

The air already had a chill, and many trees had shed their leaves, leaving glorious red and gold carpets on the ground. Guta loved the view from the entrance to the cave. He stood a few moments looking out at the long line of people slowly making their way home, but also he looked out across the wooded valley to the hills beyond and the mountains even further away, now already covered in a thin blanket of snow. Contemplating that and the deeper snow and cold to come, he shivered and turned back to make his way to his hearth. As he did so, he noticed how thin and frail his mother was as she sat on a log panting after the long climb. He hurried to make a fire in her hearth and placed some stones to heat, ready to make her a hot drink. He knew Kitam would soon have herbs steeping in hot water to make the old lady more comfortable. It was apparent this winter that Kitam would have to look after the fires in two hearths and cook food for them and his parents.

As the icy fingers of winter stretched into the cave, the clan was grateful for the protection the old Auroch skin offered from the worst of the weather. It made it dark, but better than being cold. The chill still seeped in, but the wind could only find a way around the edges, thus reducing its ferocity. The horse's enclosure at the entrance also helped to create some warmth. They were as able as the humans at squeezing around the skin curtain. The humans stacked the horse dung until it dried and then used it as fuel for their fires throughout the winter.

On days when the wind dropped, they pulled the skin curtain back and lit a fire in the main chamber where the people gathered to work on their projects. On the side opposite the horse's area were the stone nappers. They had collected small piles of suitable rough stones and struck them, chipping off flakes. The younger least experienced ones had to sit closer to the cave entrance while the experts benefitted slightly from the central hearth fire.

Both Korgai and Ivan enjoyed watching Odo, one of these skilled workers, as he worked on making hard, narrow points. Depending on the stone he was working on, he would first shape it by striking it and sending flakes off at the angle he wanted. Then he heated the stone, or if it was jasper or high-quality flint, he could use a wooden or bone hammer and press down hard on it, producing thin slivers of stone, which allowed him to control the thickness and sharpness of the tool he was making. This technique allowed him to achieve a sharper blade, especially for spearheads or knives.

They watched Odo using a long sharp point and his bow drill to make all the women in the cave bone needles with a tiny hole like Kitam had asked him to produce. Then they could all use the fine thread she had found.

Watching this, Ivan felt excited and wanted to share

this insight of pressure flaking with his colleagues. Korgai smiled, pleased to help Ivan focus on the positives again. Not the unpleasantness of one person.

The time visiting Korgai passed with Ivan learning all about the difficulties of living in a cold, hostile climate, the same as 'his' people would have faced all those thousands of years ago. All too soon, the dogs were hauling them back to the airport.

Once home, all Ivan could do was talk about the threads and the needles. Then Sonja showed him a strange fossil, not of something but the marks of a plant. Zora looked at it a long time, then said, "I think it is a plant, probably flax, but how come you found it at the back of the cave? Nothing like that grows in a cave. You must soak the plant in water until it rots, leaving only the stem fibres. Then you dry them out and spin them to make a thread."

Once again, Ivan understood what he had observed. Near Kitam and Guta's hearth, a hollow was full of water. Every few days, Kitam peered in and, using a stick, pulled up the white stuff, which he now knew as the preparation of the flax plant ready to make a thread. They had evidence, and he could explain where it came from and how those people used it.

Chapter 15

Ancient and Modern Troubles

Sonja approached the Chancellor's office, pondering what the problem could be. They had talked only a few days ago at the faculty meeting. She wondered what had cropped up now to warrant this urgent summons.

"Ah, Sonja good to see you."

Puzzled, she saw he was uncomfortable. He kept his eyes on the pad before him and twiddled with his pen. She had only seen him do this once before when he was in a difficult situation where a student had been caught cheating. She was the daughter of another academic. She assumed it must be bad news, maybe an unexpected cut to funding. "What can I do for you, sir?"

He fidgeted with the things on his desk. "How do you get along with the other faculty members?"

She jerked her head back a little and thought this a strange question, "Fine, we all get along well."

A frown creased his forehead, "Really, I've heard otherwise."

Her face creased, and her heart rate increased. That comment was uncharacteristic of him. What was going on here? In her usual tone, she said, "Sir, if there were any problems, I would be the first to inform you,"

"Well, that's not what I hear. What about that young protégée of yours? I hear he lodges with your parents. Someone suggested you have a relationship with him. You know that is against the rules."

That accusation incensed Sonja, Her nostrils flared, and she glared at him as she said, "Sir, that is ridiculous. I presume you mean Ivan. I am old enough to be his mother. I am outraged at the mere suggestion. You better tell me who has made this outrageous accusation, although I think I know who is small-minded and vindictive enough to spread this sort of poison. Would it be Yegor Morozov?"

Now he looked uncomfortable and cleared his throat, saying, "Be careful about who you are accusing, Sonja."

She was so angry she did not care what happened anymore and almost shouted, "I don't have to be careful. That weasely man insinuated all sorts of unpleasant things before Ivan came on the scene, and now he is downright rude since Ivan started here. He even accused me of trying to cheat when I dropped the boy off for his exams. He showed a bias regarding all his marking of term papers and exams. It was so bad I had to get other examiners to check up on the exam papers. He marked Ivan as a fail, yet on remarking, he came out with honours. Can you explain that?"

The Chancellor went red in the face. She was right. He knew about the papers which needed remarking. He had done some himself. That was why he thought there could be some grounds for Yegor's latest insinuation of a romantic involvement. It confused him. Was her anger genuine shock at such an accusation, or was it bluster at being found out?

He contemplated the issue regarding the papers. He had looked at Yegor's marking and agreed it showed bias and was unfair. He wondered, maybe he should not place such value on the man. He knew Yegor felt thwarted when Sonja secured the job, not him. In reality, she was the better candidate. He had to admit Yegor was not talented. He was just a plodding lecturer with little to no vision, and the post needed someone with perception and enthusiasm, which Sonja had in abundance.

He made a sudden decision and said, "Sonja, please calm down. I had to bring this to your attention. I'm sorry I doubted you, even for a moment. You have been open and honest, especially about Ivan's unorthodox methods. They have yielded more finds than usual. Maybe we need to consider these cooperative methods in the future."

She was shaken. At least the Chancellor had acknowledged she was right but to have even considered for one moment these accusations might be true made her wonder if she could trust his judgement again.

Eyes glittering with unshed tears, she stormed down to the archaeology department. She met Mikhail, "Whoa, what's wrong with you, Sonja?"

He took her arm, "Come, let's go for a coffee in the canteen. On second thoughts, let's go to that coffee shop opposite the entrance. Then you can tell me all about it."

They sat at the back but with a view out the window. Now the tears came. Like a tsunami, they flowed down her cheeks as she recounted her experience in the Chancellor's office.

He listened, getting angrier by the second, "I've had that bastard in chunks. Did you know he was so unpleasant to Ivan again recently? That's why the guy wanted to give up studying. After I told Korgai about it, he invited Ivan to visit in the tundra, hoping to reignite Ivan's commitment to studying and the cave people. Life is never fair, and we all have to put up with nastiness, but this snake is pure evil. We can only beat this by staying focused on our work and encouraging Ivan to succeed. He is the way the future is going."

She mopped her eyes, deeply breathed, and said, "Yes, you are right. Now I suppose I must get back to work and see what other things are happening." She called into the restroom and washed her face with cold water, hoping not to look like such a sight.

Things were indeed happening. Ivan was sitting on the chair in her office with his head in his hands. The very picture of misery.

Putting the recent unpleasant interlude behind her, but alarmed, she looked at him and asked, "What's the matter, Ivan? Why the long face?" She suspected Yegor had done something awful to the lad as well.

He looked strained and pale-faced as he dragged the words out. "Sonja, there's been a bereavement."

Her heart sank. She looked confused for a moment, thinking it must be one of his parents, "Ivan, who has died? When did it happen? Do you need to go home?"

He looked at her blankly. "Guta has died."

She thought a moment. What was Ivan's father's name? She was sure it wasn't Guta. Then she remembered. This was the shaman from the cave. She wanted to scream at him. These people died thirty-four thousand years ago. Why are you so upset? She caught herself in time. After all, for the last six years, he had been in contact with them regularly, almost daily. They were probably more real than his own family. Her heart rate slowed, and she contented herself with saying, "Ivan, I'm so sorry. Tell me all about it."

Ivan said, "I watched as they arrived at the Burda. Since

his father's death many years ago, Guta was the chief shaman/storyteller, so he had to attend every Burda. This year both Kitam and Chen were with him. I saw a grizzled older man hobbling with a stick coming out onto the grassy meeting place. Chen accompanied him when he told the stories, and she did all the actions, leaping about and waving her arms at the appropriate places. They worked together well in the storytelling stuff as well as in their shamanic duties. I did not realise women could be a shaman. I asked Korgai, and he said they could, but there were not many. They mostly concentrated on the healing side but not Chen. She was as powerful as Guta. They knew Kitam was there for them to do all the healing duties. We have doctors and hospitals, so why do I need to do that?"

Sonja wanted him to get on with what upset him, "So what happened at the Burda?"

Ivan took a long shuddering breath, "After the days of talking and judgments, they have a communal celebratory meal. Afterwards, everyone sat waiting expectantly, concentrating on the flames leaping up. As I watched, the drums started beating, slowly increasing in volume and pace. Then, the first storyteller leapt into the circle with a sudden crash. The entertainment had begun. The stories were wild and exciting, with each storyteller leaping, crawling, and swirling to enhance their words and their impact on the audience. Guta no longer took part in these public spectacles, preferring to sit at the side, beating the drum to regulate the story's pace. It was up to the storyteller to make his performance so natural for the audience to experience it through hearing, feeling, seeing and even smelling. A good storyteller could mesmerise their audience. At the height of the excitement, the dancing storytellers suddenly stopped. Silence reigned. No one wanted to move or even glance at their neighbours. They were so excited they could feel their blood pounding. The silence grew and grew. Guta stepped into the circle to a deafening crash from the drum when their attention was about to snap.

Smiling and clapping, the audience settled down to the most exciting part of the evening, Guta's stories. With his slow chanting voice, weaving and waving his head and hands, he began the tale, unobtrusively Chen stepped into the circle with him. They told their stories, old and new, and Chen could illustrate with all the movements they had prepared and rehearsed before. No one noticed the passage of time until the exhausted storytellers held their hands up, and the great drum beat stopped. In the sudden silence, the camp lit only by the flickering flame coming from the dying bonfire, Guta stood, arms stretched out, his black feathered cloak rustled about him as he wished them all a good night and dismissed them. Turning to Chen, he nodded and leaned hard on her shoulder. He hobbled back to his tent. The rest of the tribe silently left the circle sated with food and storytelling, retiring to their tents too."

The way Ivan recounted his experiences made Sonja feel like she was also part of the ancient audience. She prompted him, "Go on, Ivan, what happened next."

He sat there with a faraway look in his eyes, swaying slightly back and forwards, "I stayed watching as the fire died down. I felt an air of expectancy. Then it happened. In the middle of the night, after silence had settled over the entire encampment, Guta cried out and grabbed Kitam's hand. He was gasping for breath. "Quick, call Chen. I must speak to her."

I saw Kitam, panic-stricken, rush to the next tent. She called, "Chen come quickly. It's Guta. He's dying." She rushed back and cradled Guta's head in her arms as Chen tumbled in and knelt beside him. I heard him say, "You are the shaman/ storyteller now." Then with one last long sigh, he died. By now, tears were streaming down my face as I watched the Tribal leaders standing at the tent entrance, there in time to hear Guta's last words. They nodded their agreement with his wishes.

I watched as Chen and Kitam washed and dressed him in his finery. Like people paying their last respects now, all the Burda members slowly filed past his tent to say farewell. Later Chen, helped by a weeping Kitam, removed the clothing, made the appropriate red ochre signs, and wrapped him in a soft hide. The tribal leaders arrived with a couple of young men. The procession wound its way through the camp and back up the escarpment to a rock jutting out over the Birda area. They laid him down and removed the hide, leaving him open to the elements, ready for the birds to come and clean the flesh. From their talk, I understood his body would remain there until the next Burda, by which time it would just be a pile of white bones. The clan would bring them back to the cave for internment.

Ivan gave a juddering breath, Sonja, I don't understand, but this feels real. It's as if a part of me has died too."

Since it was Friday and she knew he could not concentrate on anything else for the rest of the day, she suggested he return to the farm for the weekend. Maybe meet up with Vlad and Piotr and do a ritual in the cave to say farewell to Guta. Then, he should be able to come back ready to shoulder the problems of the current century.

Vlad, now married with a small son, was glad to get time off from family duties. The three returned to their favourite spot at the back of the cave. Once a small fire was going, Ivan fished into his shaman's pouch at his belt and took out a handful of dried leaves. As the familiar pungent smoke drifted around them, they began drumming. The other two knew to continue at the same regular beat as Ivan lay down and closed his eyes.

By now, Ivan was so experienced that he quickly went

into the upper spirit world and soon saw his stag waiting for him. Together they leapt over the rocks, moving towards another plume of smoke. Ivan wondered what was causing it and had a frisson of fear. Where were they headed? He had never seen smoke before in the spirit world, although he knew the pungent smoke was a way our earthbound bodies could reach out to that other world, and shamans could travel along with it to the spirits, so why here? Why now?

Then he was back in the main cave. Kitam was looking tired and sad, her beautiful hair now all grey. Helping her was a young man who looked over at Chen. She nodded and carefully placed the parcel she carried, wrapped in a soft hide, at the back of the wall.

Ivan recognised the buzz of activity all around. They had just returned from the Birda. That parcel must be Guta's bones. He wanted to know what would happen to them now. Late that night, Chen made her way, alone, to the back of the cave. With a twinge of pity, Ivan understood she was their only shaman. He thought how lonely it must be. He hoped Guta could still help her from the spirit world. She made that squirming, wriggling journey to the hidden cave. Once there, she made her little fire, and he watched her repeat his actions by sprinkling dried leaves on it.

She was weeping as she drew the parcel of bones closer. She laid her cheek on them as if to bid them and Guta farewell. She dug a shallow hole, laid the bones to rest there, and then sat back on her heels. Ivan saw him, and so did Chen. Out of the swirling smoke was the unmistakable figure of Guta. He was smiling at her, and he also looked at Ivan. As if acknowledging the presence of the other man there too. Startled, Chen looked around. She, too, could see Ivan. She smiled a greeting knowing she would not always be alone.

Chapter 16

Discoveries Old and New

Sitting around the kitchen table in her parent's house had become the favourite meeting place of the four, Sonja, Ivan, Mikhail, and Zoya. Following the unwarranted verbal attack on Sonja by Yegor, they made a point of meeting together like this rather than on University grounds.

Also, it was not far for Sonja to travel, and she looked increasingly tired these days. Ivan had taken over all the travelling out to the cave and supervising the students. He enjoyed the responsibility and the joy when the lab techies verified any new finds as coming from "his" people. After he had told them all about his experience of Guta's death, as a group, they were more than ever determined to find the sacred cave.

Mikhail's enthusiasm bubbled over, "There's a holiday coming up soon, and I have a friend who does geophysical surveys for private companies. He flies all over the place, but I know he'll be around next weekend. What about finding out how much he would charge to come and have a sniff around for us?"

Sonja looked excited, but then her face fell, "He, whose name I will not utter, will kick up a stink about costs. I had to turn down a project he wanted us to do. I know how much trouble he can cause."

Her parents had joined them, and her father added, "Mikhail, find out how much it will cost, anyway. If it is not too prohibitive, why don't we club in and do it on our own? Sonja, can there be any objections if we approach it that way?"

"Well, it depends. If I inform the chancellor that the investigation will make an important difference and that the costs are from a private source, he might agree, we can but try."

Five vehicles arrived and parked in the farmyard the evening before the holiday. The farmer's wife showed her delight. She loved entertaining, especially paying guests, and welcomed them into her kitchen. She reserved a special hug for Ivan, "My favourite young man, who have you brought with you this time?"

The door banged open again. Vlad and Piotr stood on the doorstep, "Hi Ivan, we saw your truck arrive and thought you wanted some drumming help."

Mikhail saw them and invited them to join the council of war. On meeting everyone, the geophys friend and his assistant soon experienced the friendliness of this group of people. In no time, there were maps spread all over the table. They wanted as many sites as possible examined for their investment. The friend smiled at all these people, so dedicated to answering questions. He made a silent decision, whatever the time spent. He would not charge more than he quoted.

Early the following day, after a quick breakfast, which disappointed the farmer's wife, they all trooped out. She was hoping to provide an impressive spread but consoled herself they would all need feeding that evening, so out came her grandmother's recipe book to find a feast which would impress her guests.

Soon the expert was striding around, examining the rock near the cave entrance, searching for the storage area. There were a couple of possible sites that needed a more detailed examination. Then he followed as the party trailed off, looking for the baby burial cave. They tried a few rocky outcrops but found nothing, and Ivan was visibly distressed. "I know it is somewhere around here. I saw it and remember looking around. Those mountain slopes were clearly visible."

They did another sweep with the geophys equipment and found a hollow, which could be a cave. Ivan stood in front of it and nodded his head. "Yes, this could be it."

Mikhail, Vlad, and Piotr started digging, with instructions provided by Sonja. Meanwhile, the geophys guy had gone into the main cave with Ivan. They strode straight to the back, again where Ivan had seen the shamans going through to the sacred cave. Furthermore, the equipment showed the possibility of a cave, but there was no visible entry.

Perplexed, Ivan said, "I've seen them coming and going. There has to be an entrance here somewhere. I don't understand."

Then the geophys guy asked, "You say you are looking for an entrance used by the oldest inhabitants. What have you found here from that level recently?"

Ivan showed him the trench running at right angles to the rock face. It was about a metre deep, and they had found bone fragments there.

"If it is so deep, there is a possibility the layers have covered up the entrance. That's why we are missing it."

Ivan smiled, "Of course, I wasn't thinking about that. Can you go along the base of where we are and see if there are any anomalies? Surely the top of the entrance would be here somewhere?"

They went over the whole area again and picked up a small gap.

Ivan felt vindicated. "I'm sure that's the entrance. We must excavate and see if that gap extends down further."

Meanwhile, outside where the others were digging, they had come across a low entrance to a cave. Their dilemma was to open it up there and then or dig down slowly. Then Zora had a bright idea, "Why don't we put a phone through and take photos? Depending on what we see will direct what we can do."

Sonja was pleased with that idea, so they were busy trying out this idea when Ivan arrived. None of the photos showed much. Then they put the torch on one phone to light up the area and used another phone to take pictures.

Sonja peered at the results and yelled, "I can see a body there."

They all crowded around to see and agreed it was a body. Now, if this was an ancient one, it needed handling with great care. Sonja decided the wisest course of action was to seal it safely again and mark its location. Then she would arrange for a specialist team to come and examine the area and see if it was safe to remove the body.

Weeks later, the specialist team removed the body and transported it back to the labs in a special coffin, but they also dug into the cave floor and found a few bones and a green bead, which they also brought back.

The minute Ivan saw this, he said, "That is Kitam's mummified body, and the bead shows that it is her baby. We must do DNA to prove it. The clothing is like the ones I've seen them wearing at the Burda. It even has the white beads at the ends of the fringe. Like the bead, we found at the back of the cave. I think that is where Guta made the hearth for her when they married. Also, I saw that green bracelet on Kitam when she arrived at the cave right after her marriage, and I saw Guta bury the bead with his son."

Sonja was sure he was right. However, they had to go through all the proper channels of investigation to prove him right.

That night Ivan did his shamanic ritual and was transported to the cave. He saw Chen had married the young man who had helped her carry Guta's bones back. She had two small children sitting at her hearth, too, so life had been kind to her, and he saw Kitam, bent and grey-haired now but holding the little one on her lap. Ivan was pleased. To her knowledge, she had not had children of her own, but at least she had the pleasure of grandchildren.

He saw she died peacefully in her sleep. But Chen, instead of allowing her mother to go to the deathrock, had undertaken all the usual care of the dead. Such as washing and anointing her with red ochre. However, in a departure from tradition and with no explanation to anyone why, she had dressed the old lady in her wedding finery. Her soft doeskin tunic, mocassin, and even her beautiful green bracelet, which had been so admired by the cave women when she first arrived. She then wrapped her body carefully in a soft bearskin pelt before she and her husband carried the body to the little cave. Many years ago, Guta had told her about the loss of the baby boy and where he had buried him. Chen thought Kitam's spirit would finally meet up with her son. They could find Guta and travel in the spirit world together. She sealed the cave with melted beeswax, so nothing in this world could disturb her beloved mother.

Ivan watched Chen as she went through that difficult passage into the sacred cave. He noticed she always lit the fire and added the dried leaves. Ivan wondered if the smoke helped her journey, but he also thought the firelight might have made that place less frightening as she was alone. As he watched, she called upon the spirit of Guta and told him why she had placed Kitam with her baby. He appeared to approve. She then drew more images on the cave wall. They were rather strange, and Ivan deduced she was showing the resolution in the spirit world. The figures did not look like real humans. Instead, they looked elongated, almost stick-like.

This double discovery once again caught the eye of the media. The press was after a quick story, but the academic world was also excited. The attention meant Sonja, assisted by Ivan, was very busy. No one noticed how pale and tired Sonja was. Well, if they did, it was all put down to the pressure of the find.

Fortunately for her, it happened while they were all at their usual kitchen conference. She was talking and suddenly passed out, slumping forward onto the table. Ivan and Mikhail rushed to her side and gently carried her to the lounge, placing her on the sofa. While her mother phoned for an ambulance, Zora held her hand as she came round, "Where am I? What happened?"

Zora looked worried but smiled, "I think you have been overdoing things. You fainted. Your Mum has called an ambulance, though."

Sonja shook her head, "I don't need an ambulance. I'm fine now." She tried to get up but was too weak and flopped back again.

It was not long before the paramedics filled the room, two tough-looking guys and all their equipment. After they had completed their investigations, they said she had to come back with them to the hospital. Her mother went with her while the rest of the party followed. When they found parking and walked into the hospital, the emergency team assessed her and sent her for an urgent scan.

They all sat hunched on the seats, waiting. They were all afraid of what this meant for Sonja. It looked much more serious than just overwork. They sat staring at the clock, waiting for the doctor to come and tell them what was happening. He did, and they wished he had not. The consultant admitted her immediately. She had a brain tumour and needed more tests to discover what was happening.

Poor Ivan felt this was a nightmare and a punishment. After being offered the opportunity to follow the shamanic healing path, he rejected it in favour of contacting the spirits. The spirits in "his" cave. Now he felt helpless. How could this happen to such a wonderful person as Sonja? He thought he had let her down by not being able to help her. He said as much to Mikhail.

"No, Ivan, you have not let Sonja down. She is so proud of you and what you have achieved. She thinks this blending of two different disciplines could change how things work in the future. Whatever happens to Sonja, now you owe it to her to keep going the way the two of you planned. You know Zoya and I will give you whatever support we can. Now stop being so melodramatic. Look, I can see the nurse beckoning us. Let's see what news they have now."

A few weeks later, pale-faced Sonja came into work.

Chapter 17

An Ivory Tiara

They stood chatting before heading off to their respective offices when Zoya gasped and grabbed Mikhail's arm. "Look who's here!"

He spun about, and they watched a moment before hurrying to catch up with Sonja as she slowly walked down the corridor. They linked arms about her to give her extra support as she hobbled like an old lady. Her pallor also appalled them. Zoya said, "Sonja, it's good to see you, but surely it's too soon for you to be back at work?"

She smiled tiredly and said, "I'm getting bored at home. My professor said I could come back for a couple of hours so long as I don't tire myself. I wanted to see what has been happening in the department. I have had no reports from Yegor since I've been off sick. My secretary usually sends me a message to say she has logged all incoming letters and reports. There is total silence from that troublemaker. Ivan came over yesterday. He's been brilliant, regularly coming to tell me about the encounters with his 'people' and keeping me updated about the activities at the two cave sites. I don't know if you know I've moved in with my parents since my discharge from the hospital. Strangely, I'm in the room where Ivan used to live. You know he's moved into his flat?

He's sharing with Amaana, the eldest of the sisters. She started at the university this semester."

Zoya linked arms with her friend. "Yes, we knew about his flat. Truthfully, we helped him move in while you were still in the hospital. He and your mom thought it best for you to return to them. It's done Ivan good to be independent."

Mikhail hurried ahead of the girls to open the office door and ensure Sonja's comfy armchair was ready.

"Thank you so much, Mikhail. I'm fine, but I need to sit a moment to get my breath back."

Zoya said, "Do you mind if I sit with you for a bit? I've got an irritating student who keeps bugging me. She can't decide about anything. She is always darting in to ask simple questions."

Zoya looked at her friend as Sonja leaned back in the chair and closed her eyes.

The aroma of fresh coffee and cinnamon buns wafted into the office. Mikhail and Ivan stood at the door carrying laden trays. "I bumped into Ivan, and we decided it was coffee time."

Sonja opened her eyes and smiled to see all her favourite people in the office.

Ivan handed her a cup of coffee while Mikhail proffered a plate as he said, "When you've had your drink, I think we better escort you home."

There was a buzz in the room as they chatted like old times, but no one could miss the deterioration in Sonja. It had taken all her strength to get here, much less get any work done.

A slight figure stood on the threshold, glaring at the assembly of people. "I heard you were home. You don't look well enough to be here, or are you all plotting your next salting of objects at the cave site, ready for your caveman to find before you die?"

There was a horrified silence before Mikhail roared. "Get out of here with your unpleasant insinuations before I flatten you!" He strode across the room, pushed Yegor out, and slammed the door.

* * *

At Ivan's home and the work sites:

Bone was getting old and spent his time grazing close to the house. He was still in residence in the lean-to at the warm end of the house. While the other sheep, there was a fair-sized flock now, had a shed to keep them safe at night and provide shelter during the worst of the winter weather. Ivan's dad had built it and monitored the flock, but when they needed to go up into the pasture, he used a young boy to watch over them.

Meanwhile, the valley sites where the mammoth hunt occurred had yielded several arrowheads and spear points. The mere fact of finding them was significant, but there were two distinct styles of manufacture. This led Sonja and Ivan to believe the hunters came together for this hunt but lived and made their points at different sites. The second cave they had opened was where the superior arrowhead maker worked. But, interestingly, the spear points from the main cave were better. The archaeologists finally decided that these differences must result from two nappers, one from each cave, rather than a change in the general method of manufacture. Ivan's descriptions of the distinctive appearances of the visiting hunters and the local ones lead the archaeologists to conclude these were two different tribes. They supposed the tribes collaborated in specific situations and married into each other's communities, as proved by the weaver, Aiee, and her husband, Een, the clan leader.

Ivan also noticed the other tribe wore their hair differently, tied back or wound into a knot. In contrast, the people in "his cave" wore their hair loose. Controlled by a band on the brows and tied at the back of the head. One day there was great excitement among the workers when a strange ivory "ornament" was found towards the back of the cave, but at the deepest level. The object, carved from a mammoth tusk, was curved, about 8 inches long and an inch and a half wide, with holes at each end. The excitement at the discovery was electric. Everyone who saw it had a suggestion regarding its use. As the holes showed considerable wear, most thought it was a form of a belt. Unable to make a definitive identification, it lay in a drawer for quite some time.

One cold, damp Autumn day, as the leaves swirled down and the rain pattered on the windows, Sonja stood in the office and opened the drawer on one of her visits. She had often looked at the strange piece of ivory, but today she felt drawn to it. "Ivan, what do you think this could be? It looks like a rawhide fitted through the holes at each end. There are distinct wear grooves which lead me to conclude it is a form of clothing used daily too, but unlike everyone else, I can't imagine what it is."

He towered over her now. He had grown since they first met, but Ivan was sure she was shrinking, or maybe it was because he felt so protective of her since the diagnosis of her illness. He took the strange object and, running a hand over it with a thoughtful look, said, "I think I need to go to the cave and make a journey from there to see if I can find anything out about it."

Ivan was happy to take her out to the farm. They laughed at the change. Now he was driving her, and he was no longer that shy young lad but a qualified man with a full-time job in the department, and she only came in when she felt strong enough.

Ivan helped Sonja into the farmhouse, where she sank gratefully onto one of the kitchen chairs beside the warm range. The farmer's wife bustled around and made tea as she pulled a delicious-smelling cake from the oven. The farmhouse had undergone many changes since that first day Sonja had arrived, calling for Ivan to show her where he had found the bone. There was a substantial wing with two big rooms for the students and single rooms for guests. As Ivan was almost a permanent fixture, he had a room for which he paid the farmer a small rent. It was convenient, as he could store stuff here rather than dragging equipment back and forth. Also, there was an efficient heater in the room. Ivan smiled, recalling the small, cold place where he had started this journey of discovery. Piotr made sure he also had a cosy room now, with none of the privations Ivan suffered. Sonja waited in the kitchen while Ivan ensured the room she would stay in was warm and comfortable. Then he went back into his room for a moment to look around and remember how full of life Sonja had been when she came that first time. Now, however, she insisted on coming. He could see she was tired just from the journey.

"Sonja, why don't you stay up here while I check what's going on in the cave? You could even have a lie-down, and I'll come for you later. They planned for her to join him on one of his trance journeys. She wanted to be with him as he went to find out how the owner of that piece of tusk used it. They did not think there was any religious connotation, as there did not seem to be any markings on it. They assumed it had an everyday use. While down on the dig, Ivan had arranged for Vlad to come down to the cave that evening and see if Piotr could join them, too.

The three men, bundled up with warm clothing, carried all the stuff they would need: drums, blankets, and wood for the fire. Once set up and the fire going, Ivan returned to the farmhouse to collect Sonja. She wore a full-length beaver-lined coat and thick boots to ward off the chill air. As another insulation from the cold cave floor, he put wooden boarding with a chair on it for her.

While waiting for Ivan, the brothers practised their drumming. They chattered, "He fusses over her like she was his mother, not his employer."

"Vlad, what a stupid thing to say. She is a kind of mother. She gave him this new life. Think about it, that silly lamb and a bone lead to all this." He waved his hand around at the scaffolding and the deep trenches branching off in all directions.

Vlad nodded in agreement. "Yeah, you're right, and we can't complain about the changes in our lives either, all because of her." He was thinking about his permanent job here, in charge of security and supervising the explorations. In this cave and at the other one, the arrowhead cave, as they called it. He was also grateful for the little cottage, which kept his wife and son safe and warm.

Ivan appeared with Sonja holding onto his arm. Looking at her gaunt appearance sent shock waves through the brothers. She was so thin and looked frail tucked into her warm coat. When the greetings were over, Ivan settled her into the chair and tucked another rug around her. Meanwhile, Vlad put more wood on the fire. Ivan had agreed to work with firelight this time, but Piotr said he could turn the lantern off once they started.

They drummed softly at first, creating an air of expectancy. They all knew why Ivan was undertaking this ritual. Well, at least they thought they did. He had told no one but Korgai. He wanted to contact Guta and ask him for help with Sonja. She was aware of the drumming. Sonja relaxed into the warmth of the coat and chair. She felt as if her body was reverberating to the beat, too. Her eyes closed, not something she had intended.

Next, she was gently floating along. Below her, the land was lush and green. She saw banks of spring flowers spilling down in a riot of colour, yellow, white, pink, and blue, with a few red ones for emphasis. She saw no one about but experienced a deep sense of safety and of being loved. She smiled, thinking this was a dream, and then she saw Ivan hold out his hand to her. In this dreamy state, she took hold of his proffered hand. They travelled together along a deep valley and up a slope into a cave. Green creepers screened the entrance like a lush curtain. At a casual glance, no one would think anything was behind the dangling greenery.

Gently Ivan led her into this cave, but way back in the mists of time. A slim man with greying hair came to greet them. She looked at him. His pale blue eyes sparkled, and his long light brown hair was held in place by an ivory plaque across his broad brow and tied with rawhide at the back of his head. He seemed to exude gentleness, yet he was confident and sure of himself. He led her to a place at the back of the cave. Where an older woman was making a drink, Sonja saw her using the stone and basket method, just as Ivan had described. They offered her a rock to sit on and gave her a warm drink. Almost immediately, it took the dreadful headache away. Sonja had not told Ivan how much pain she was experiencing. Otherwise, she thought he would not have brought her out here.

She watched Ivan and the older man walk into the shadows far to the back of the cave. They were there one moment and then disappeared. This would have frightened her any other time, but she knew that was the way into the sacred cave. She tried to peer into the blackness to see if she could identify it another time, but once again, she felt as if she was floating, but there was nothing to see, just a deep sense of peace.

She did not know where she was when she felt a firm hand on her arm. "Sonja, are you all right? Have you been asleep? It's time for us to go back to the farmhouse."

She looked up and saw his concerned face. She smiled, "I came with you, didn't I?"

He nodded. "Yes, as I was setting off. I was aware of you, so I came and took your hand and brought you here, but long ago."

She grinned as she said, "I know, that was Guta, wasn't it? He was wearing the mammoth ivory plaque. Now we know who wore it and how and why. I accepted a warm drink from Kitam too. Was that one of her herbal concoctions?"

Ivan felt his heart rate increase. He, too, was grinning. He didn't know he could do something like this, but Sonja had come with him! She had met these people to whom he felt such a strong affinity. "Yes, it was Kitam. Did your headache go after you took it?"

Her eyes widened, and she clutched her hands together. He could see she was shocked. In a low tone, she said, "How did you know about the headache?"

With a lop-sided grin, he shook his head and said, "Sonja, I've known you for a long time. You can't fool me when you're in pain. I can see the lines all over your face, and your neck muscles are tight. Is it better now?"

She nodded her head. "Yes, but now I'm exhausted. I think it's time we went back."

It was his turn to laugh. "You are back. We carried you in the chair. Look about the place. See, you're in the kitchen."

Touched at their thoughtfulness, she smiled. "Ivan, thank you so much for everything, but I want to go to bed now."

The following day, the sky looked ominous. The clouds spread over the sky like bruises after a boxing match. Looking out the kitchen window, Ivan frowned and called,

"Sonja, I think we should leave soon. The weather looks bad. I reckon we'll have snow by this afternoon."

Sonja came out a few minutes later. She looked better and said she had slept well. Relieved, he wondered if it was the stuff Kitam had given her. While he loaded the vehicle, Sonja swallowed a quick cup of coffee, and the farmer's wife packed them a picnic breakfast. She could not bear to think they might leave her house feeling hungry.

After they pulled out of the rutted farm track onto the main road, huge fat snowflakes fell. Ivan was grateful he had put the new winter tyres on last week. They drove in silence. He was concentrating on the road, and she on the events of last night. As they pulled up to her parent's house, he felt a sense of relief. It had taken much longer than the usual journey, but at least he could drop her off in the strange grey-green pre-snow daylight. Her parents hurried out to help her in.

Her mother fussed over Sonja, "Thank goodness you made it back. The forecast is dreadful, heavy snow for the next three days." She thought of Ivan as family and turned to him, saying, "Can you make it for dinner this evening with your sister too?"

He nodded. "Of course, we'll walk. That way, it won't matter how much snow falls. But I won't be able to make it into the department. I'll write a report on the visit and email it, so Mikhail knows what's happening."

Sonja nodded and walked up the path. Her father watched, then turned to Ivan. "You know, she looks a little better. What happened out at the farm?"

Ivan smiled to himself. "Oh, nothing much. I think she needed a change of air."

The older man looked at Ivan. "I don't believe you. This evening, you will get questioned to the nth degree, so be prepared."

Ivan accepted that and drove slowly to his flat to tell his sister they were going out that evening.

Chapter 18

Snowy Explorations

After a lovely meal, Sonja and her Mum, together with Ivan's sister Amaana and Zoya, left the menfolk to clear up as they went to sit in the lounge. This arrangement was so Sonja would not feel as if she was letting anyone down. From the sound of raucous laughter coming from the kitchen, the men were having fun washing up and making the coffee, anyway.

At last, they came in with trays full of coffee cups, the coffee percolator, and delicious pastries, which Ivan had seen earlier as he walked around to the house in the swirling snow. He thought it would fill any empty corners left after a lovely meal. Also, as they all sat and talked late into the night, an extra bit of sweetness went down well.

Sonja looked over to Ivan, "What are the results of the geophysics explorations?"

"Well, you were there when we found the burial cave, so that was positive, but there was nothing conclusive about the storage cave or the sacred cave. I know they are there, so I suspect we need to dig a trench alongside the cave wall at the back to look for the sacred cave. You know where we were this time."

She nodded and looked wistful, "Pity we have to wait until spring to do any more exploring."

Both Ivan and Mikhail understood what she was implying. She might not be around to see what lay in that cave.

Mikhail looked over at Zoya, who gave a slight nod. Then he went on, "Well, as soon as it stops snowing, I would like to go out again and look for that storage cave. To hell with waiting until spring. I want to follow the lines from the geophys exploration and try tapping the rock, we won't be digging, and we can do it on the weekend, so it will be under the radar as far as the department is concerned."

Sonja smiled, "Well, only if Ivan goes too. If you find anything without him being there, I won't hear the end of it."

She had not realised that it was just the response they wanted from her. Then they got onto the latest results from the laboratory. Since it was quiet, as there was not a deluge of finds to sort and date, they did DNA analysis on as many human bone fragments as possible, including the original thigh bone Ivan had found. This analysis was a massive undertaking as there were over a thousand fragments. Still, the lab boffins thought it might help to understand the people's connections, if any, between the layers.

Two days later, with the snow settled, Ivan, Mikhail, Zoya and Amaana crammed into his truck. He had good winter tyres, and they had no difficulties getting there. Of course, once again, the farmer's wife enjoyed having guests. She confided to Ivan that the winter evenings were very lonely without him there studying. Ivan's dad said he would drive to collect Amaana so they could use all the available time working.

As the battered old truck pulled into the yard, his dad

yelled out the window, "Well, my boy, what are you planning to do this weekend? Are you hoping to make even more discoveries? Your Mum says she thinks there is something in the air, I told her it was just the snow, but she insists you are on the verge of another great find."

Ivan walked over with his sister, who jumped into the truck, "Dad, we are only following up on what that geophys guy located. By the way, how is Bone doing?"

"Yes, it was after that geophys stuff you found the cave with the mummy in it. I'm sure there was other stuff, so your Mum could be right. There's still room for more. Ah, Bone," the old man smiled, "he is doing fine, but he is getting old now. He doesn't go far from the house, and he waits for me to bring him a bucket of feed every morning and evening. You should come and see him sometime."

Ivan nodded and waved to his family as they drove off.

The three of them struggled down to the cave entrance through deep snow. It made Ivan think about his people. They lived in a time when the weather was much more severe, yet they showed ingenuity and foresight. Mikhail and Zoya made their way to the back of the cave to light a fire, but Ivan sat in a pensive mood at the entrance. He wanted to locate both the storage cave and the sacred cave as soon as possible, knowing the prognosis for Sonja was so bleak. He wondered if he was ridiculous, wanting to find stuff before she was likely to die.

As he sat thinking and his eyes were unfocused, a trickle of water ran down the rock, and then it disappeared. It took a moment for him to register what had happened. Now he stared closely and watched as another drop followed, doing the disappearing act too.

"Mikhail, Zoya, come and look. There's something odd going on here."

They hurried out, concerned, then looked where he was pointing. They, too, watched a drop of water make its way down and then disappear. It worried Zoya. She knew Ivan was despondent about the news concerning Sonja, "Ivan, are you feeling all right? It's a dribble of water. What's so amazing about that?"

Ivan continued, "Look at the path it's tracing. It is going over solid rock. Then it disappears. How? There has to be a gap there."

Mikhail looked again, "Yes, it's going into that mossy area."

By now, Ivan had jumped down and landed up to his waist in a snowdrift. As he tried to climb out, his feet found purchase on a solid rock ledge. Clinging to the side of the rock face, he reached the green patch and patted it, no water. "The moss is not absorbing the water."

Mikhail was excited by now, "Then it must go in."

The import of what he had just said hit him, "Oh, I see what you are getting at!"

By now, Ivan was standing on the rock and running his hand over the surface, "I can feel a bit of a crack here."

Instead of jumping down as Ivan did, Mikhail gently put his foot out until he felt something solid: the rock ledge. "You said you saw them move along a ledge. Do you think this is it?"

Zoya chuckled, "Will you guys be careful I don't want to dig you out of a snowdrift on my own."

Two voices called out in unison, "You won't need to. We're here now. What's going on?"

Zoya looked relieved, "Thank goodness, you've arrived. Vlad and Piotr, these two are looking for a lost drop of water."

The new arrivals looked puzzled, "What did you say? How can they lose a drop of water?"

Ivan explained about the drops of water.

"Ah, yes, I see what you are getting at. Wait while I grab a ladder, a couple of hammers, and a lever." Vlad returned to the cave, and besides the other items, he returned with some ropes too. By lowering the ladder into the snowdrift, they had a safe place to stand. With some manoeuvring, Ivan moved onto a rung of the ladder. Without the fear of slipping into the drift, he took the hammer from Vlad. He gently knocked as they all listened. Below the mossy patch, there was a hollow sound.

"I think we might have found a cave. It could be the storage cave!"

They all took turns scrapping the moss and lichen away. Then they could see the faint outline of a break in the rock, where the drops had been traversing in their disappearing act.

They got a little of the lever into the crack. With lots of heaving, it grew a little wider. The guys all took turns trying to budge it, and then Zoya called, "Why don't you try going down the sides, I think that is the top you are working on, and I remember Ivan saying there were two rocks which came out. If we could identify if this is the left or the right-hand rock, you would have a better chance of moving it."

They nodded in agreement and started looking for a side crack. A few inches down from the "top," they located a slight gap on the right side. They all took turns pushing and levering sideways until, suddenly, the rock moved. Vlad was on the ladder at the time and had such a shock he fell into the snowdrift. The others quickly pulled him out, and they all sat by the fire to dry him out and warm up a bit.

Suddenly they heard Zoya call, "Hey guys, come quickly.

I think it's the storage area!"

The cold forgotten, they hurried out again. Zoya was perched on the ladder, shining a torch through the crack they had just opened. They all took turns to peer in and agreed this looked like the place Ivan had seen in his trance and later described to them.

Back at the farmhouse, they talked, "I was an idiot when the geophys guy was here, and we were looking for a ledge. I saw it deep in winter with snow everywhere. We were looking there with no snow, so we didn't see a ledge. It was above us!"

Vlad murmured, "You saw it but described it to us, and no one thought they were living in the cave because that's where they were in the winter, and there would be snow, lots of snow. As far as I remember, it's never been this deep."

Mikhail said, "Well, we've located it, but how do we explore it?"

Zoya answered, "I think we need to get that robot thing to go in and look around. It can relay what it sees in real-time. I think it would be interesting to see what, if any, fossils their food has become."

Ivan slowly answered, "We need to examine the back wall of this part of the cave and dig a trench before we go for the robot. They are expensive, so I'd like to find the site of the sacred cave before going down that expensive route."

Vlad asked, "Where were you planning on looking? What if Piotr and I scrape around here? Then if I see any signs of a break in the rock, you could come over, and we could trench it. I presume you want this done before the students are here?" Ivan appreciated his diplomacy in putting it that way rather than mentioning anything about Sonja.

"Yes, that would be great."

Vlad was glad about the idea of some physical work, and he knew Piotr felt bored looking after the sheep in the shed. Vlad had worked with Ivan for so long now he knew how careful they needed to be. Also, he was more than capable of dealing with any finds. Only he knew they would not send them to the University just yet, as the site should be closed.

They all put in a couple of hours of work the following day while Ivan drove over to see his mother and collect his sister.

As they dug along the main cave's back wall, Zoya found some bones, not scattered around but in distinct piles. "Do you think this is where they buried the bones after the death of a cave member? I remember Ivan said they took the bodies out, then later brought the bones back. I'm sure he said he saw them buried after being marked with red ochre."

Since Mikhail and Ivan were technically the head of the department, he decided, "We can take a few bones back for the lab to check. I know they are not too busy as they are doing DNA testing. We could always say we found them at the bottom of a drawer in Sonja's office. We only need to imply she had missed handing them to the lab."

Once again, they sat around the kitchen table to brief Sonja on all their discoveries. She also admitted to not thinking about the winter weather way back then. It would be awful, so of course, the ledge would be "higher" than where they had the geophys guy search. They told her about Vlad and his brother offering to check out the back of the long arm or, technically, the south chamber of the cave to see if there were any signs of the entrance to the sacred cave. She smiled, "Those guys are enamoured in the same way as Ivan is about these ancient people."

Chapter 19

Dilemma

The printer was churning pages that fell to the floor as thick and fast as the snow outside. Ivan and Mikhail were peering at the screen of the computer.

"We should contact these people first."

Ivan shook his head. "I think this company has more flexibility."

Zoya came into the office and looked around with dismay as more sheets flew off the printer. "Ok, now guys, you should stop all this printing and think first."

"But, we want to show Sonja."

"I know what you want, but if you take this mess, all you'll give her is another headache. Why don't you stop now? Collect this mess into an intelligible document, talk it over and when it's clear in your minds, then take it to Sonja."

They looked like a pair of schoolboys the teacher had just told off.

Soon there were piles of paper for companies offering robotic solutions for many complex issues, but none could respond to what they needed. The food storage cave was relatively simple, but getting into the sacred cave was a much more difficult problem. For a start, they knew the site of the storage cave. But regarding the scared cave, they were only in the early stages of establishing where it could be. Vlad had carefully removed soil all along the back of the South chamber of the cave. However, he had still not seen anything which might hint at the fissure where Ivan had so often seen the shamans of old squeeze through.

The phone rang, Ivan answered, and they all heard the excited voice at the other end, "Guys, I think you'd better come out and see this. I've just found a small gap in the back wall. It could be the top of the fissure!"

They looked at each other and grinned, all thoughts of sorting out the paper forgotten. Zoya shrugged as she picked up the haphazard mess and stuffed it into a folder to deal with later. She knew they would dash round to Sonja and then go to the farm, whatever the weather. Knowing them so well, she grabbed her coat and bag and locked the door, followed as they clattered down the stairs. Yegor came to the door of his office and asked what the matter was.

She knew he wanted to cause trouble. She smiled and replied, "Don't worry, it's nothing important. There's a water leak at Ivan's flat."

He looked crestfallen, "I heard them talking about a robot and thought they had found something important."

She wondered how he could have heard what they were talking about and thought she would have to see if it could improve the security. She was glad she had grabbed all the papers up into the folder. Which was now in her bag as she also hurried down the stairs.

Once at the Solokov's house, the men started talking at once.

Sonja looked pale and weak. She had endured a

chemotherapy session all morning, and all she wanted was to puke and sleep, but the guys were so excited. "Do you think you could both speak softer and slower? I don't have a clue what you're going on about."

Suddenly they looked at her. Ivan noticed her pallor, "Oh my god, Sonja, I'm so sorry we didn't think. We came rushing here to tell you what was happening, and I didn't even ask you how you are feeling. I'm so sorry. Can we start again?"

She smiled at him, acknowledging his contrition with a slight nod, "Yes, I'm sorry too. I had chemo this morning, so I don't feel on top of the world. What do you want to talk about?"

Both men started together again until she put her hands up, "Hold it, one at a time, Mikhail first."

He looked at Ivan, "No, we have so much to tell you. I think Ivan better start."

Ivan smiled at her, "Vlad has just phoned to say he thinks he has found a crack in the cave wall, which could be the top of the fissure I saw Guta and his father pass through often. I think it best we see it for ourselves before digging any deeper. Would you like to come?"

Sonja looked at him. It seemed her eyes had grown even larger, although maybe it was just the weight she had lost which made it seem so. "I would love to, but I don't feel up to all the jolting. Why don't you guys keep in touch with me by phone?"

Vlad was waiting in the yard as they arrived, and Zoya had stayed behind with Sonja. The three men walked through the swirl of falling snow, taking care of where they stepped along the path to the cave. Vlad had rigged up a strong light directed onto the rock face at the end of the cave. Ivan paced back and forth, trying to recreate the topography of the entrance area to the sacred cave in Guta's time. He knew it was further back than any of the dwelling areas. Try as hard as he could, the proportions did not come to him. As he accompanied the shamans in a trance state, there were no steps to take.

When he felt he was at the right place, he asked Vlad to show him the crack. It was just to his left. That was in the correct position! They all knelt, peered at the rock, and then dug down at the spot. Since no artefacts were here, they hoped they would not destroy too much.

They dug with a trowel, a gentle prod into the soil, loosening the earth and finally lifting it. All done slowly and carefully. Each of them took turns digging while one carefully sifted the soil in case there were any precious fragments. The others peered at the rock surface. The crack extended down, and slowly, they could see it widening. Now they were all excited. Ivan's heart was pounding, his adrenaline going into overdrive. Was this finally the entrance to the sacred cave?

He stuck his finger down into the soil to feel and confirmed the space was still getting wider. They carried on their slow, methodical labour until there was a pyramidal-shaped gap about a foot long.

Vlad called, "Ivan, I think you better do this bit. I think I can feel the gap getting wider."

They all watched as Ivan carefully lifted another spoonful of soil. Some of it fell into a space.

Vlad was ecstatic. "Ivan, I'm sure there's a space behind. You've done it!"

Mikhail handed Ivan a phone, "See if you can see inside with the light."

Ivan peered for a few moments, then sat back on his heels. A wide grin split his face, "I think this is the way into the cave. It's a longish passage with a kink. Then the opening is very low. You crawl into the cave itself."

They took turns peering into the hole. There was no doubt the floor was deep below them and led off into the darkness.

Mikhail asked, "Ivan, did they need to bend to get into it?"

"No, but it was narrow. They had to squeeze in sideways. Then it opened out into more of a passageway, but with that kink."

"We would have to go down quite a way to reach the floor level. How are we going to get a robot in there?" Asked Mikhail.

Ivan smiled, "There was a company that had robotic drones. Maybe we could fly it along?"

Each explorer felt a sense of elation. This was the way to the sacred cave. They needed to shore it up before leaving the cave in case anything fell in. They also agreed not to mention it to anyone apart from Sonja and Zoya. They were on their guard after Yegor's comment to Zoya as they dashed off to Sonja.

Vlad decided he needed to increase the security at the site. Besides the usual security, he laid out an elaborate system of tripwires linked to lights and bells. If a mouse ran about, it might get away, but nothing bigger and certainly no human.

His precautions were justified. The next night alarm bells started going off in the middle of the night, and lights lit up the site so brightly it was like daylight. The man apprehended was a small weasel-faced creature with wispy ginger hair when he removed his black balaclava. At the first sound, Vlad rushed over and found this miserable specimen of a man trying to escape. When questioned, he said he did not know the person who paid for him to come and take photos. Vlad did not believe him and happily handed him over to the local police with a reputation for not handling suspects gently.

Meanwhile, the usual crowd had gathered at Sonia's. They decided in the future to conduct all their meetings connected with this new level of exploration at her place but to continue everyday activities from Ivan and Mikhail's shared office. They suspected somehow, Yegor might have bugged the office. Sonia's mum Sofia had an office in the firm of architects she worked for as well as one at the university. Sofia offered the use of her architect's office for all the international communications regarding robotics and anything relating to the site other than everyday activities. In case Yegor had set up surveillance of their actions, they put out that Sofia was working on designing a prominent building in Dubai. That way, no one would think anything odd about her coming and going carrying files of paperwork. Instead of gathering in the kitchen, they made Sonja's old bedroom another office, with laptops and printers, all with inbuilt heavy security.

When Yegor noticed Ivan and Mikhail were spending time at Sonja's, he assumed she was deteriorating and informed the Chancellor.

The following day the Chancellor visited Sonja. It surprised him to find her alone and looking a little better. He accidentally mentioned that Yegor thought she was worse since Ivan and Mikhail spent time with her.

"Oh no, Yegor must be wrong, they pop over here after work, but I don't see them during the day. I wonder what made him think they were here?"

Confused, the Chancellor blustered, "Yegor said he saw them coming here, though."

He had not noticed she had a little buzzer in her hand and was pressing it.

A few moments later, Sofia came into the room.

She feigned surprise, "Oh, sorry, I did not see you had a visitor, Sonja." Looking at the Chancellor, she smiled, "Can I get you a drink? Tea or coffee? I might even have a biscuit or two hidden away. When Ivan and Mikhail come over after work, they always bring something tempting for Sonja, then set to and eat whatever it is!"

He looked confused, "I called into their office, and they were not there. Since Yegor mentioned they come here often, I thought I might catch up with them here."

Sonja smiled wistfully, "It would be good to see them during the day, but they all have jobs to do, so I have to wait until the evening."

"Ah, if you see them this evening, let them know I would like to chat with them about work."

He had not noticed the two men sneak past the now-closed door of the lounge.

As they hurried out the backdoor, they split up and agreed to meet at their office. That way, if there were any surveillance people posted outside, it would not be easy to follow two of them simultaneously.

Back at the university, Yegor closed the office door as Ivan came from one end of the corridor and Mikhail from the other. He looked one way, then the other, confused.

Smiling, Mikhail asked, "Hallo Yegor, how did you get into our office? What or who were you wanting?"

Ivan quipped, "Were you hoping to find out about the man arrested at the site trying to take photos?"

Yegor's face reddened, "I don't know who or what you're

talking about."

Now Ivan sounded menacing, "Oh, I think you do. The policeman took him to the local police station, and in return for a little warmth. Ok, they left him chained up outside in a snowstorm for a while. The police are so absentminded out in the country. Anyway, I think the phrase is, he is singing to them."

Yegor shook his head, "I don't know who or what you're talking about. Why should I care about anything you do? You make up most of the stuff coming from that site, anyway. I just wanted to prove that you plant stuff there. I've heard you talking."

Mikhail growled, "Really, how can you hear us talking, anyway?"

Yegor was sweating now. Both Mikhail and Ivan saw the beads popping out along his brow. The two men towered over him, and he began to feel scared, "Oh, you know, as you walk along the corridors and in the canteen."

Mikhail clenched his fists. It was apparent he was ready to swing a punch. At that moment, the Chancellor hurried along, "Ah, Mikhail, Ivan. I'm so glad to see you, where have you been? I called round earlier, and Yegor here said you were with Sonja. I went there, but she said you don't go until the evening."

Mikhail let out his breath and relaxed his fists, "I don't know where Ivan was, but I popped over to see Zoya about a new fossil she has identified."

Ivan glared at his old lecturer with undisguised hatred, "I did not know I had to ask Yegor if I could go to the labs. More importantly, how and why was Yegor coming out of our office since I know I locked it when I left? Maybe, Chancellor, you would like us to move into our office. I wonder if Mr Morozov would be kind enough to unlock the door since he has the key in his hand."

Yegor still had a key in his hand, and with three pairs of eyes boring into him, he fitted it and clicked the lock opening the door for them.

Ivan put his hand out, "And now, please drop your copy of our key into my hand."

Yegor had to obey, and they all moved into the office, but not before some of Yegor's students witnessed the little scene. They piled out of his office since he was supposedly giving them a tutorial. Sniggering, they escaped to the canteen. Yegor knew that within minutes, the whole story would circulate throughout the student body, no doubt with some embellishments.

However, there was no sniggering in the office, but there was a simmering. The Chancellor headed for the big comfortable chair Ivan and Mikhail had installed for when Sonja came in to visit. They sat at their desks and left Yegor to sit in front of them on a less comfortable chair.

The Chancellor looked at them, perplexed, "Could someone explain just what is going on here? This is a university, a place of higher learning. There is no room for squabbling, especially if it is at the expense of the reputation of this place. Ivan, you can start by expanding your statement about a man singing."

Ivan spoke, saying nothing about their discovery of the entrance to the sacred cave or their considerations relating to the use of robotic explorations. He mentioned their uneasiness after they had to rush out to fix a leak and Yegor's comments saying he had heard them talking. Since then, they had called in an expert who had identified a few bugs in the room, all feeding back to Yegor's office. As a result, they increased security at the site. Shortly after, the police arrested a man trying to gain entry. He had several items in his pockets, stolen from the university museum. Although ancient, they were not from the era of most significant interest. To the police, the man confessed his instructions were to scatter these items in the cave towards the back. He described the person who had hired him, and it fitted with Yegor.

The Chancellor put his hands to his head, "No, no, this cannot be true." He raised his head and looked at Yegor haggardly, "Please tell me you haven't done this."

Yegor had the decency to look shamefaced, then decided they knew so much there was no point in denial. "It's not fair. All those years ago, you passed me over and gave the job to Sonja. I have watched her help this farm yokel," pointing a finger to Ivan, "cheat his way through the system. Now she's sick you give him and Mikhail the job which by rights should be mine."

Horrified, the Chancellor said, "Sonja got the job because she was the best person. It was not a decision made by me alone. The whole board interviewed you and her, and it was their considered opinion she was the better candidate. I don't know why you object to Ivan, either. He had to sit entrance exams the same as many others and scored very well. He had to study the same curricula as everyone else. I know there was no cheating. You consistently scored him low, so I had to intervene and remark his work. Did you hear me? I did all the remarking. Sonja was unaware of my intervention. There can be no suggestion of cheating. Ivan gained his degree fair and square."

As the Chancellor continued, Yegor seemed to shrink into the chair. He looked so defeated that Ivan allowed himself a moment of sympathy.

Yegor raised his head. "He cheats all the time, goes off to sleep and comes back with so many fanciful ideas. It's just luck there have been any real finds."

The Chancellor glared at this small-minded man, now, two red patches appeared on his cheeks, but he controlled his temper, "If you are referring to his using shamanic techniques to guide the investigations, I have to admit I was wary at first. Now I am convinced this is how archaeology needs to go, not just here with him. Maybe you are unaware, but there's a growing body of evidence where shamanic archaeologists have had great success at digs worldwide. I am sad you have sunk so low as to salt artefacts into a site, and your behaviour in bugging this office is shameful. I presume it's your son who did that job for you. I'm afraid I have no option but to dismiss you with immediate effect. You'll accompany me to my office, where I will go through the administrative steps to make your dismissal immediate and permanent."

With those words, he rose from his chair, nodded at the other two and stalked out, followed by a defeated Yegor who glared at them and hissed, "You haven't heard the end of this."

Mikhail breathed out and looked over to Ivan, who was looking exhausted.

"Come on, pal, let's get out of here for a while. We can come back later. First, we need to get a locksmith to come and change the keys. Then we need an electronics engineer, not Yegor's son, to come and clean up any bugs there might be left. I know just the person in the electronics department."

Ivan nodded and followed the older man out of the office, his thoughts a maelstrom. He knew Yegor disliked him, but this was at another level altogether.

Chapter 20

The Power of Suggestion

There was a knock at the door. Ivan went to open it and standing on the step was his sister. "Ivan, what happened to you at the university today?"

"I thought you said you had a tutorial this evening. What are you doing here?"

"How can you expect me to go to a boring old tutorial when such exciting things are happening to you?"

He looked genuinely puzzled. "Tell me what exciting things are happening. No one seems to have told me."

She looked at him a moment. "Are you going to let me come in? It's cold out here."

"Sorry, come on inside. We were talking to Sonja."

"I bet you are. There's such a lot to report to her. While you bring her up to speed, I'll sit and listen."

When she sat instead of listening, they questioned her. According to the rumours, Yegor had gone into their shared office, and Ivan attacked him. Mikhail had phoned the Chancellor for help, and it had taken the two of them to stop the fight. Yegor had come off worse and had to go to the hospital. Besides his physical injuries, Yegor experienced such psychological trauma he probably could never return to work.

Ivan laughed. "My, I didn't know I was so strong. What damage did I inflict, Amaana?"

"No one seems to know for sure that's why I thought I'd find out. Then I can tell everyone tomorrow."

Mikhail looked a bit worried. "But that's a load of lies. Who's spreading these rumours?"

Sonja looked at him. "Yes, we know it's lies. We must look at who comes best out of this pack of lies. Then we'll know the source."

"Well, put like that, Yegor comes out best, like a saint even, while Ivan is the farm boy bully." Commented Zoya.

Sonja nodded her head. "Precisely, if Yegor is not there physically, who do we know who is a close friend? They're responsible for propagating this rubbish."

They all sat thinking while Amaana looked from face to face, and then Ivan's face lit up. "I know, that woman at the canteen, you know, the one who takes the money. She hangs on every word Yegor utters."

Sonja smiled. "So, there's the source. In one stroke, it explains why Yegor is not at work and puts Ivan in a bad light."

Ivan looked distressed, "That bloody man, he's as slippery as an eel. He's insulted me and belittled me all the years of my being a student. Now I'm qualified, he still tries to make me look the baddy. Meanwhile, he's free to cause me more trouble. I wish I had hit him. He deserves it."

Sonja smiled. "Don't get emotional, Ivan. Let's come up with a plan."

They sat talking for hours, but not before sending

Amaana to her tutorial with a little story to spread amongst the students.

The story she was to spread was this. While Ivan had been in the shamanic trance state, he had seen Yegor in a distant place where he had found a rare new fossil. They had invited Yegor into their office and informed him about this unique situation. He was so excited he asked for leave with immediate effect from the chancellor. The suggestion of violence on either side was a lie. In fact, Yegor was very grateful for the opportunity to improve his professional career.

Although Yegor was no longer on the premises, they were still aware of the danger of spies and the cooperation of Sacha, his son. To maintain their secrecy, they continued working from the different sites. Also, they wanted to be near Sonja and share each new step they took into the robotic arena with her.

Spring brought so much activity a couple of different vehicles parked in the farm yard went unremarked by most people. However, they excited Ivan, who hurried out to greet them. "Hi, I'm Ivan." He stuck out his hand, and a beautiful brown-haired woman shook it. She was wearing dungarees and looked ready for any kind of work.

"Hi, Ivan, I'm Stella. These are my brothers Dan and Tommy. Five years ago, I started working in robotics with an emphasis on AI."

Ivan looked confused. He had worked in farming for years and was familiar with AI. What could this lady do which made her suitable for robotics?

Stella saw his confusion and looked around at the farmyard, "Oh, of course, you would think artificial insemination. The AI field I work in is artificial intelligence, hence the robots!"

Ivan's face cleared, and he nodded understanding while she continued, "Dan here has an electronics engineering degree, and Tommy has a degree in aeronautics. We pooled our abilities to form our own company. I do the design work. They do the building. We all get to play with our toys."

Ivan blinked a moment, then shook the two guy's hands. It was easy to remember them. Dan had a beard and blinked owlishly through thick pebble-like glasses. Tom was clean-shaven. Ivan could see the familial similarities in their smiles and how they moved their hands.

They made their way to the entrance of the workings. However, after all the trouble Yegor caused, Vlad, insisted they went through a full security check before he allowed them onto the site. His insistence on security bordered on paranoia. Nothing, and no one could enter the site without his approval. The cases they carried were of particular interest, but he thought it would be safe only if he were with them all the time too! Another man wanting to play with grown-up toys.

The party arrived just before lunch. All the students and workers had gone up to the farmhouse for their break by the time the group reached the entrance to the cave. They scrambled along the scaffolding to the site of the storage cave. In situ, they opened their cases, unpacked, and assembled some strange-looking equipment. It looked a little like those remote-controlled toys children received for Christmas, only this was bristling with antenna and lights and, of course, its fully operational battery.

While they were assembling this peculiar contraption, Ivan and Vlad were loosening the entrance stones. Dan carefully lowered Bobby, the robot, into the entrance.

Then he looked at the group, "Right Ivan, Bobby here is ready to probe the deep dark secrets in this cave." He handed Ivan a remote control button, "Since this is your site and your secrets, you better be the one to tell Bobby where to go and what to look for."

As he was about to press the button, there was a shout, "Hang on Ivan, Zoya and I got away after all."

It seemed fitting that Mikhail and Zoya would be with Ivan on this first foray into another field of discovery. One which they helped to bring about.

Dan explained. "We have designed these robots with cameras that transmit what they see, and we can see the same images on this screen." He pointed to the screen on the inside of the case lid. "This way, we can direct Bobby to any special area of significance. Normally we set Bobby to move in a grid first, so we have an idea of what is there. Then you guys can decide what and where we go. Also, Bobby has pincers and can collect into the basket anything you fancy."

Everyone peered at the screen after Bobby was let loose into a space that had not seen the light of day for thousands of years. Zoya was particularly interested in this cave as foodstuffs would inform the archaeologists what these hardy people ate. Zoya hoped to find the remains of the food that sustained these hardy people over the punishingly cold winters.

Bobby moved around doing a quick circuit before slowing down and scanning in a slow grid, which it recorded. Zoya made a note of anything unusual. Then they planned for Bobby to go back and take close-up photos for Zoya to study later. Bobby also had tiny pinchers, which allowed the operator to work remotely. This manoeuvre they planned to do in the morning to harvest any exciting material after Zoya had looked at all the photos.

True to his capabilities, Bobby, following instructions from Zoya, collected a little basket of ancient titbits.

Meanwhile, the others gathered at the area they were now sure was the entrance to the sacred space cave. Ivan explained to the mystified robotics experts. "I know this has to be the entrance to the sacred cave as I have seen it often in my shamanic trance, as has Korgai. They looked doubtful and wondered if this was a wind-up, but everyone appeared deadly serious.

He explained. "We are looking for the cave used by the original inhabitants who lived here about thirty-four thousand years ago. This main cave has had occupants almost continually since then. The stuff left on the floor slowly accumulates. From our trenches in other areas of this cave system, we know the floor we need to reach is about 6-7 feet down. I know this is only a tiny gap, but we are sure this is the entrance passage. We need your drone to fly along, negotiate a bit of a kink, drop to ground level, and go through a small opening into the sacred cave. I'm hoping that if you get into this cave with your feedback images, we should see the paintings done way back then."

He knew if they could prove the paintings' existence, they could get funding to continue the exploration. Then it would be worth excavating down to the original floor level. The three experts were excited to be trying out their new flying drone in such a meaningful search.

Dan and Tommy explained. "For this site, we will use Batty, our flying drone. Yes, Ivan, like Bobby, we have that same feedback system, so you will see exactly what Batty can see. We can then tell her what you want her to do."

Ivan removed the soil again to reveal the hole they had peered through.

Tom asked. "Ivan, could you open the hole a little more so Batty can fit, please?"

Ivan nodded. " Yes, of course, we can make it a little

bigger, but I am afraid of stuff falling in if we make it too big."

"That's ok. We only need a little more room to squeeze Batty's wings through."

The device fitted the entrance, and Tommy activated the mechanism. Then sang out irreverently. "Watch out, you old guys. Here comes the new world."

They all watched the screen. Ivan held his breath. Batty flew along slowly as if it was taking in the scenery. It went past the kink, and then Ivan yelled, "Down to the ground now that's where they crawled through."

Tommy guided the drone as it went lower and lower, but they could see nothing, just the cave wall.

Ivan was so tense. After all this, the cave has to be there. Surely there couldn't be a rockfall now!

Then Batty went a little further along and dipped down again. Ivan let out his breath. He didn't realise he was still holding it. There on the screen, was a low entrance. They all cheered.

Batty flew slowly down and went into the sacred space, which no one had seen for thousands of years. The scene took their breath away. They all saw the walls covered with the paintings, just as Ivan had seen them. The others were dumbstruck. There were so many images. It would take a very long time to study them. But there was also a bundle on the floor which he had never seen. Long and thin, it seemed like rolled-up rawhide.

As well as showing on the screen, there was also a camera on board to record all the sights.

Ivan was so emotional tears streamed down his face. Vlad held his shoulder, "Come on, big guy, at long last, we're getting to see what you've experienced all these years.

Best of all, you can take the film back for Sonja to see and experience."

Once the filming was complete, and Zoya had her samples, the three engineers packed the robots into their cases. It was late, and Ivan wanted to return and show the film to Sonja, but reason won the day. It was a long drive and better done in the morning. They stayed in the farmhouse, but apart from saying they satisfied the experts, none knew what momentous events had just unfolded.

There was paperwork that needed attention. It was not till late in the morning before Mikhail, Zoya, and Ivan set off for town. Ivan was so excited he wanted to share everything with Sonja as soon as they got back. The team rushed to the house, but it was dark and silent. The three of them looked at each other, and Mikhail said, "We've only been away a couple of days. She was looking better. Now, what's happened?"

Ivan was frantic, "She must have had a relapse. We'd better go and see." They hurried to the hospital and ICU. By now, Ivan's heart was beating so fast he was sure it was as loud as his drum. Sonja's parents were sitting in a waiting room, looking tense.

Ivan burst out, "What's happened to Sonja? Why is she here?"

Her father patted him on the shoulder, "Hush, lad. Come with me to the canteen, and I'll explain while Mum stays here."

He was seated on one of those uncomfortable plastic chairs. Ivan looked at the old man questioningly, "What's going on? You look worried."

Her dad nodded. "I've bad news for you. After you left, Sonja had a fit. We phoned the hospital, and they sent an ambulance in minutes. She has had a scan. There is a bleed on the brain. They don't hold out much hope. Come, I'll take you to her now, but be quiet."

Ivan found it hard to take in. She looked so well when they left; now Prof Sokolov said this. Just when they had discovered the sacred cave. He felt like screaming and tearing his hair out.

As they walked along the corridor, Ivan said, "Is there nothing we can do to help her recover? I've been feeling so guilty. After Korgai said I could become a healer, and I refused, Sonja became ill, and I could not help her. Whatever she needs to help her recover, I'll be there for her. She's been like a mother to me all these years. Now I can be there for her, help her in whatever she needs."

Her father smiled grimly. "Ivan, you need not feel guilty, but she will be very glad of your company now."

They entered the sideward, where Sonja lay covered by a sheet accentuating her pallor. It shocked Ivan. She had gone down so quickly.

He held her hand and whispered. "Sonja, it's me, Ivan, I've just got back from the site, and I wanted to show you the most exciting film."

She grasped his hand and amazed everyone as she opened her eyes. In a soft voice, she got out a few words. "Ivan, I knew you'd come. What do you want to show me?"

With shaking hands, Ivan held the phone, so she could see the images. He tried not to let any tears show. Then the images flickered across the screen. A smile spread over her face. Her hand still held Ivan's. "Ivan, now I see what you've seen all these years. That bundle on the floor looks like a body, like the mother and child one."

Ivan nodded. "You mean Kitam and her baby? Yes, I think you're right, but I wonder who that is. I've never seen them take a body in there. But, come to think of it, I saw

Guta take his father's bones in and bury them, and I'm sure Chen would have done the same for Guta. I wonder if they bury the shaman's bones while all the others are at the back of the East Chamber? I must get in physically to confirm, but I guess it's Chen."

Sonja looked radiant as her parents stood on one side of the bed, and Ivan held her other hand. "Ivan, you've got a lot of work ahead of you, and I need you to look after my folks too. I'm tired now and need to go to sleep." Her gaze took in all the others standing at the foot of the bed. "I love all of you."

Her eyes closed, and her breathing slowed as she slipped away from them.

Hours later, at the Sokolov house, they sat looking at each other. It was hard to accept she had gone. The phone rang. It was Korgai, "Ivan, I saw Sonja passing. She gave me a message, She's thrilled seeing into the cave with you, and she will be with you as you continue to work there. I'll come down when I can get out and I'll see you then."

Chapter 21

Travel

After a few weeks, Zoya marched into their offices. "Right, guys, I've had enough of seeing your long faces. We're all going out to the cave to have a party to celebrate all that Sonja did there and what she meant to us. I've someone who needs to go out there too."

She indicated, and Korgai came into the room. He was shocked to see how thin and drawn Ivan looked. The man was the picture of misery itself.

"Hi guys, I'm sorry I couldn't get away when our friend passed into the spirit world. A small thing called winter had us all snowed in for weeks."

Days later, a long line of vehicles left the town heading to the site. Waiting at the farmhouse were all the regular folk, the farmer and his wife, Vlad and Piotr, and some of the workmen and students. It surprised Ivan to see his parents lined up to meet him and the rest of the crowd too. Korgai caught their attention, dressed in his shamanic finery. Ivan's mother put her hands over her mouth, "He looks like the old man from my village when I was a girl."

Korgai smiled and went over to her. "My name is Korgai. Do you know the name of the man you were friends with as a child?"

She stammered out an answer while going red in the face. "His name was Bukdur, an old man, but when I left to get married, he gave me those pouches Ivan has now. I think he was a shaman, like you and Ivan."

Korgai looked at Ivan. "Maybe when we go on our journey, we can plan to meet this man and Sonja."

Poor Ivan could only nod. Still immersed in his guilt at what he felt was his failure to help Sonja and misery at her loss.

The farmer's wife called out. "Come in out of the cold. Hot drinks are waiting for all of you."

Ivan's mum hurried in to see what she could do to help. She had never had things done for her. She always did the work. The farmer's wife recognised a fellow worker, and soon, the two of them were chatting as they poured tea and coffee and plied everyone with cakes.

Korgai whispered to Ivan. "We will have to see if Vlad will allow us to go to the cave to make a spirit journey. I'd like to know more about this man Bukdur that your mother knew. Where did she live as a child?"

Ivan remembered the name of the village but had to admit he did not know where it was as they had never visited it while he was a child, and she had never talked about her childhood.

Soon the noise in the kitchen rose. Ivan wanted quiet, so he went to his room and sat on the bed, feeling miserable and cut off from everyone. Then he heard Sonja's voice in his head. It was the conversation when she persuaded him to study the entrance course. He heard her say, "You're a smart kid." At that moment, the door creaked open, and his mother put her head around.

"Come, Ivan, the others are looking for you. I'll talk to you later."

He reluctantly rose and went back to the kitchen, which was emptying as they all dispersed to get on with chores. Korgai looked at him. "Come, my friend. We also have some work to do."

They sat by the little hole, which was the entrance to the sacred cave. Soon they had a fire, and the pungent smoke took them off to the other world. Once there, Ivan saw his stag looking up at the eagle, Korgai. They journeyed to a strange place, and traces of mist trailed ahead of them like a smokescreen. On the other side, they saw a beautiful land with green rolling hills and a riot of exotic-coloured blooms. The sound of birdsong was sweeter than Ivan had ever remembered. Where was this? They had never visited this place before. Then he saw her, Sonja, smiling and walking towards him with arms outstretched. "Ivan, it's so good to see you again. Don't pine for me, this is a beautiful place, and I can see what you're doing all the time."

That made him laugh. "I hope not all the time!"

She smiled. "No, you idiot, not every moment of the day. I have things to do here, too, you know. I want you to understand that this was meant to happen to me. The best thing was you found the sacred cave and showed me before I came here. Korgai says in the same way as you used to visit Guta and all the others, you can visit me too."

Ivan wanted to touch her, but she shook her head. "We can talk and observe, but I cannot touch you nor you me. I want you to know you are like a son to me, and I'll always watch over you."

"I'm so sorry, Sonja. I failed you when you most needed me. I never learnt to do any healing."

She laughed. "If anyone could have healed me, it would

have been Korgai. It was my time. We all have to learn that. So stop this silly guilt trip you're indulging in at the moment. It's not doing you or anyone around you any good."

The trails of mist seemed to thicken, and the beautiful view with Sonja waving faded. Ivan was back in the spirit world with his stag, where he could see the Korgai eagle swooping down. Soon the two of them were travelling in another terrain Ivan had not visited before. "Korgai, where are we going now?"

"To visit a colleague who knew your mother."

Like when Ivan visited the people of the cave, this old man was sitting on a tree stump banging his drum. He had his eyes closed and was chanting. He looked up as they came closer and beckoned them to join him. It surprised Ivan that this man was also of the same tribe as Korgai. He was a Yugur shaman but had left when he was young and had never acquired his power animals or his spirit guardian. As soon as Ivan's mother had mentioned the name, Korgai remembered the stories of a man who fell in love and left their traditional land. They sat beside him. When he saw the pouches hanging from Ivan's belt, he recognised them as the ones he gave to the young woman leaving to get married. He grinned a wide toothless smile to show his approval. "Those were mine a long time ago. I'm glad I was right feeling your mother would pass them to someone in the tradition."

They sat in companionable silence until Korgai stirred. "I will visit you again, and maybe Ivan can come too if he has time. Farewell, friend. You are not alone anymore."

They were rewarded with another toothless grin.

Later Korgai told Ivan, "When he left to marry that girl, he had to give up his shamanic activities. The authorities banned any such activities. It turned out his wife was horrid, so he lost everything. When she died in childbirth, it relieved him from the constant nagging, but he felt ashamed to come back to us. I'll visit him now and again since I've made the connection. He might yet join us in the spirit world. He can learn things there too."

Things were not going smoothly for Ivan. A prestigious journal printed a scurrilous paper accusing Ivan of salting (hiding objects to be later found) the finds from the cave. It caused such a furore in the archaeology world there were serious, learned folk wanting to visit and the gutter press who were always glad of the scent of trouble.

Mikhail stood frowning and tapping his finger in the palm of his hand, a favourite gesture when he was uncertain of anything. "Ivan, why are they mentioning finds we have not made public yet? Have you spoken to anyone?"

"No, I've not mentioned anything." He grew thoughtful. "Amaana has a new boyfriend. I wonder if there is a leak there? She should ask me if she can bring anyone to the flat."

The two friends went back to the flat. It looked as neat as always, but Ivan's briefcase was at the side of the desk in the lounge. Mikhail picked it up, and it fell open. "Ivan, what are you doing with this lying around unlocked?"

Ivan's eyes grew huge. "That's my work one, it should be in my room, and I know I left it locked."

Mikhail signed to be quiet and signalled they should leave. They went over to the Sokolov's house before speaking. "Ivan, something is going on in your flat, and I bet you there is a bug or two there too. I'll call my friend to come and check. Meanwhile, get Amaana to come here. We need to talk to her."

When Amaana arrived, she looked shocked to see her brother and Mikhail looking angry. "There's no need to look at me like that. I came as quickly as I could. What's wrong?"

Mikhail opened his hand, and lying in the palm was a little button thing, "This is what's wrong young lady."

"I don't understand what is it and what's it got to do with me?"

"It's a bug, and someone planted it in the flat you share with your brother. Are you trying to destroy his career?"

She burst into tears, "I don't understand, I've never seen that before, and I would never do anything to harm my brother."

Ivan stood up and crossed the room to stand before his sister. "I'm glad to hear that, but someone has been in the flat. They have bugged the lounge and my bedroom. Picked the lock on my briefcase and moved it from my room to the lounge. Do you know who that could be?"

She looked wide-eyed at the two men. "The only person who has been in is Sai when I went to change before we went out."

Ivan sounded threatening. "I presume this Sai is your boyfriend. Where does he work? What does he do? How long was he alone in the flat?"

Now she was sobbing. "He works in engineering at a firm in the city."

The men looked at each other. Ivan said, "Does his surname happen to be Morozov?"

She looked up. "Yes, how did you know?"

Mikhail snorted. "Do you know who he is? Do you know what type of engineering?"

Amaana looked afraid. She had never seen Mikhail or her brother so upset and angry. "I, I don't know much about him. He met me at a nightclub. He says he likes me."

"I bet he does, his name is Sacha, not Sai, and he is the son of Yegor. He is the one who bugged our office. Do you know what you have done?"

She shrank down into the chair and, in a soft voice, said, "I didn't know all that, I promise. I only left him in the flat for a few minutes while I changed. How can he have bugged the place?"

Ivan was still angry but knew it wasn't Amaana's fault Sai had used her. Both father and son were unscrupulous men.

When the Sokolov's came home and they heard about the bugging and the article. Prof Maxim immediately said, "Ivan, I think you should move into Sonja's flat immediately. That will take care of the security issues. Amaana, don't say a thing about Ivan moving out to that snake of a boyfriend. Let's see what he does now."

She was so upset she wanted to tell him to get lost there and then, but the others decided to play him along. They had a friend set up another bug and a tiny camera to feed sound and images to a computer in Ivan's new residence. They also replaced Sai's bug, but only after Ivan's removal had happened. They organised a friend with a cleaning company to call round to the flat and clean as a distraction for the removal of all Ivan's things, especially his papers.

After another meal, they all sat around the table to discuss the way forward.

"I'd like to find that ass Yegor and beat him up for what he's accused me of doing."

Prof shook his head, "No, Ivan, you know Sonja would say don't give in and respond emotionally. You'll fight this the academic way."

"Oh, and how do I do it that way?"

Mikhail jumped up. "I've got it! Why not go on a lecture tour? Talk about the cave from the beginning to now, even hint about the sacred cave. Create a thirst for the secrets yet to be revealed. You could do this in Sonja's memory."

Sophia Sokolov said, "You know I think that is inspired. Don't mention Morozov or his outlandish accusations. They are beneath you. Show the images you took for Sonja, make the world sit up and look at the wonders you have found with your unusual gift and the latest technology."

For a moment, Ivan looked hopeful, and then his face fell. "I don't speak other languages, only Russian."

Mikhail said, "That's not a problem. There are always interpreters, and now those apps convert one language into another. I'm not sure how reliable they are, but an interpreter would be great. We could speak to the Chancellor and tell him what we are thinking. As well as what that slimeball Morozov and his son have done to your reputation and your personal space."

* * *

Ivan flung his suitcase on the bed in yet another hotel. "Zoya, thank goodness you could join me for this part of what feels like endless hell. Hall after hall filled with people gazing at me. I feel like a fish in an aquarium. Not to mention all the newspapers and news services asking stupid questions."

The young woman laughed. "Mikhail has been watching you on all the replay tapes. He says you're an inspired speaker. I bet there will be queues wanting to join archaeology courses, most hoping to get to drink that magic potion. What's it called?"

Ivan sighed. "It's called Ayahuasca, made by the shamans in South America, although I believe there are places in the west where you can go for parties or something and take it.

It's not for me. Korgai uses nothing, and he is one of the most powerful shamans alive today, so why should I? I do remember Kitam gave something to Guta, though."

Zoya picked up the pile of newspapers. All splashed with similar headlines. "Drone confirms modern shaman's encounters with a new branch of ancient humans after his sheep finds a bone in a cave."

She said, " You've done so well. You've obliterated those stupid accusations of Yegor at the same time as fuelling interest in more exploration and a novel approach to archaeology. Mikhail says they've had to take on extra staff at the university to answer all the calls and offers of funding or people."

Ivan smiled. "I'm so pleased but so tired. I want to go home so badly. Thank goodness you've come to join me on this last leg of the tour."

"That's only because you've got people curious about what they ate in those days. I'm not sure we know all about their diet, but after the finds in the larder cave, we know a little more. And there's the discovery of the flax, too. Come on, let's go down to dinner. Do you have any meetings this evening?"

They sat chatting over dinner, Ivan still did not like to drink, but Zoya was enjoying her glass of wine when a lady approached. "Excuse me, sir, but are you Dr Ivan Yezhov?"

Ivan looked up at yet another face and wondered what next. He swallowed. "Yes, I am. Can I help you?"

"I'm not sure. I work in communications and wondered if you have ever thought of writing a book?"

Zoya interrupted. "Even if he wanted to, he does not have the time at the moment."

The lady looked up, "I'm sorry I did not mean to

interrupt a private dinner. You are?"

Zoya laughed. "I'm Dr Zoya Konev, a paleo ontologist. I'll be joining Ivan for the next part of the tour to talk about the fossilised foodstuffs and other things we found in the cave. My husband works with Ivan. He's a paleoanthropologist."

The lady looked impressed. "You are all highly qualified, but I read an article about Dr Yezhov, where the writer claims you are just a farm boy, and the finds are all down to luck."

Zoya's face flushed red. "Did you now? If you want to repeat lies like that, we have nothing more to say, and maybe you should leave us."

Ivan squirmed uncomfortably in his seat, unsure how to manage this situation. "Excuse me, what is your name, and where do you work?"

She stood back, looking at them for a moment, then said, "I'm sorry we seem to have got off on the wrong foot. My name is Dora Collins. I run a publishing company. Could I make an appointment to talk to both of you? I think there is an opportunity to write a book about your discoveries and, pardon me for saying it, your unusual techniques to find these objects."

After that stormy start, they got on well. They tentatively arranged for Dora to visit the university, which led to long conversations and emails between the three of them and Maksim and Sofia Sokolov, both for their personal skills and being Sonja's parents. The result was to be a beautiful book about the journey Sonja had started Ivan on and her help and inspiration. They all agreed it was a fitting tribute to Sonja. Dora regularly visited to produce the book and promote it, causing Mikhail and Zoya to wonder if there was a growing attachment between her and Ivan.

About the author

Like a rolling stone, Felicity has lived and worked in Kenya, Queensland, Rhodesia, South Africa and England.

A fascination with ancient rock art started when young in Africa and has never abated. This led to studying archaeology alongside her physiotherapy career and now retired she has the time to read and research the many aspects of ancient people in different settings worldwide.

She lives in the Forest of Dean, Gloucestershire, with one little black dog for company.

Printed in Great Britain
by Amazon

19415089R00123